Not eve[...] d lots of players can start out like Jamie in this story – not sure which position to go for.

Others [...] want to [...] everywhere! This friend would run all over the pitch to get at the ball and he'd always bring a ball with him to school. In the end, we just used to expect him to provide a ball. If he was off sick, or hadn't brought it in for some reason, none of us could play footie at break time! If you like playing, I bet you know someone just like him.

Keep playing and practising. Why not have a go in another position too? You might surprise everyone!

*Theo Walcott*

A NOTE FROM THEO

## Access your secret bonus content!

Every Theo Walcott T.J. book has SECRET

bonus content online. It could be a cool

download, football tips, a secret story . . .

or something even more exciting!

Check it out at:

**www.theowalcottbooks.co.uk/penalty**

**Also available by Theo Walcott:**

*T.J. AND THE HAT-TRICK*

**Coming soon:**

*T.J. AND THE CUP RUN*

*T.J. AND THE WINNING GOAL*

# THEO WALCOTT

## WITH PAUL MAY

# T.J. AND THE
# PENALTY

| WARRINGTON BOROUGH COUNCIL | |
|---|---|
| 34143100389293 | |
| Bertrams | 07/07/2010 |
| JF | £4.99 |
| CUL | |

## ILLUSTRATIONS BY JERRY PARIS

CORGI BOOKS

**T.J. AND THE PENALTY**

A CORGI BOOK 978 0 552 56246 1

Published in Great Britain by Corgi Books,
an imprint of Random House Children's Books
A Random House Group Company

This edition published 2010

1 3 5 7 9 10 8 6 4 2

Copyright © Theo Walcott, 2010
Illustrations copyright © Jerry Paris, 2010

The right of Theo Walcott to be identified as the author of this work has been asserted
in accordance with the Copyright, Designs and Patents Act 1988.

Theo Walcott®™ is a registered trademark and is owned by TJW Promotions Limited.

This book is a work of fiction. Whilst real events have inspired the author, the
descriptions of such events, the characters, actions and conversations of the characters,
and the names of places are entirely the products of the author's imagination.
Any resemblance to actual persons, events or places is entirely coincidental.

All rights reserved. No part of this publication may be reproduced, stored in a
retrieval system, or transmitted in any form or by any means, electronic, mechanical,
photocopying, recording or otherwise, without the prior permission of the publishers.

The Random House Group Limited supports The Forest Stewardship Council (FSC), the
leading international forest certification organization. All our titles that are printed on
Greenpeace-approved FSC-certified paper carry the FSC logo. Our paper procurement
policy can be found at www.rbooks.co.uk/environment.

**Mixed Sources**
Product group from well-managed
forests and other controlled sources
www.fsc.org Cert no. TT-COC-2139
© 1996 Forest Stewardship Council
FSC

Set in 14/22pt Meta Normal

Corgi Books are published by Random House Children's Books,
61–63 Uxbridge Road, London W5 5SA

www.**kids**at**randomhouse**.co.uk
www.**rbooks**.co.uk

Addresses for companies within The Random House Group Limited can be found at:
www.randomhouse.co.uk/offices.htm

THE RANDOM HOUSE GROUP Limited Reg. No. 954009

A CIP catalogue record for this book is available from the British Library.

Printed and bound in Great Britain by CPI Bookmarque, Croydon, CR0 4TD

# Squad Sheet

**TJ:** A skilful forward with an outstanding turn of speed. He has an incredibly powerful shot, and he's good in the air too.

**Tulsi:** A strong, powerful striker. When she has the ball at her feet all she thinks about is scoring!

**Rodrigo:** He's from Portugal and he doesn't speak much English, but he's a wizard with a football in midfield or defence.

**Rafi:** A midfielder who never stops running and tackling. His mazy runs are legendary and he always brings a ball to school!

**Tommy:** When he's not skateboarding he's a fearsome tackler in Parkview's defence.

**Jamie:** A big, strong defender. It's almost impossible to get past him, but when he clears the ball it could go anywhere.

**Danny:** He's not popular, but he's a terrific defender and Parkview can't do without him.

**Ariyan:** He can play anywhere and do a good job for the team. A really useful squad member.

**Cameron:** He plays in midfield or defence. Always works hard and almost never gives the ball away.

**Rob:** The team statistician. He dreams about being a footballer, but he's too nervous to join in training.

**Leila:** She's new to football, but she always stays calm under pressure. She can play in defence or midfield.

*FOR MY MUM AND DAD*

A special thanks to Caroline McAteer and
Pippa Hancock from The Sports PR Company
and Jonathan Harris from Luxton Harris Ltd

# CHAPTER 1

'Can I get you some more, Jamie?' Mr Wilson asked.

'Yes, please. This is really great, Mr W. I think it might be the best thing I've ever tasted!'

TJ's dad grinned. 'I knew you'd like it,' he said. 'Everyone does. It was my granny's favourite recipe. Lamb and peas.'

TJ watched his friend Jamie tuck in to his second helping. They were supposed to be going to the park after lunch for a kickabout, but if Jamie carried on like this he wouldn't be able to move. 'Watch it, Jamie,' TJ said.

'People sometimes eat so much of Dad's food that they explode!'

'Right,' said TJ's big brother, Joey. 'They swell up like enormous balloons. They get bigger and bigger and then—'

'Leave him alone,' said Lou, TJ's sister. 'The more he eats, the stronger and hand-somer he'll get. Like Matt.'

Jamie blushed. TJ sighed, as he saw the dreamy look in his sister's eyes. Lou had been going out with Jamie's brother, Matt, since the day they'd all helped to mend the football pitch at Parkview School three weeks before.

'Come on, Jamie,' TJ said, as Jamie gulped down his food.

'We'll be late.'

Jamie groaned, as he stood up.

'I warned you,' TJ laughed. 'You're going to burst.'

'I don't care,' Jamie said, as they left the house. 'I'd eat it all again, honest I would. Thanks, Mr Wilson. Bye.'

When they reached the park the others were already waiting. Tulsi and Rodrigo were sitting on the swings. Rafi was riding on a roundabout while he tried to do keepie-uppies with his head. On the far side of the park TJ saw Tommy's red hair rising and falling on the ramps in the small skate park.

Rodrigo grinned when he saw TJ. 'Good,' he said. 'Now we can match.'

Rodrigo was from Portugal. He had started at Parkview School six weeks ago, at the beginning of September, on the very same day as TJ.

'Now we can *play* is what you mean,' Tulsi

said. 'I've been teaching Rodrigo some new things,' she told them. 'Go on, Rodrigo.'

Rodrigo paused, trying to remember. 'You need a glass, referee,' he said.

'Aaaagh!' Tulsi held her head in her hands, as they all laughed. 'I keep telling him. It's glasses! Like Rob wears, see.'

She pointed to where a small curly-haired boy was coming through the gates. He was wearing huge spectacles with square frames and carrying a large notebook.

'Oh, yes,' said Rodrigo. 'Referee needs glasses.'

'Better,' said Tulsi, as Rafi jumped off the roundabout.

'We're wasting time,' he said. 'We should be playing football. Me and TJ against the rest of you. Rob can be our goalie.'

Rob shook his head. 'I have to concen-trate,' he said. 'I can't keep a proper record of what happens if I'm playing.'

'It's just a kickaround—' Tulsi began, but TJ interrupted.

'It's up to Rob,' he said. 'He's our official assistant coach, remember?' They started to argue about teams, but then TJ saw a bunch of kids arriving on bikes. 'Look,' he said. 'Hillsiders.'

'What are they doing here?' Rafi said. 'I thought we'd scared them off.'

They hadn't seen the kids from Hillside since they'd beaten them in their first proper match as a school team a couple of weeks ago. 'We knew we'd find you here,' said the tall black girl who was their leader. Krissy Barton was the top striker in the Under-Elevens league. 'We thought you might want a game.'

'Sure,' said Tulsi. 'We'll beat you any time you like.'

TJ looked suspiciously at Krissy. Then he looked at the other Hillside kids and realized that one of them was new. 'Who's he?' he asked, pointing at the skinny Chinese-looking boy at the back of the group.

Krissy shrugged. 'Who, Deng?' she said innocently. 'He's just a new kid. D'you want a game or not?'

'We'd better watch him,' TJ muttered to Jamie, as they got ready. 'Krissy's up to something. I bet Deng is really good.'

Tulsi passed the ball to TJ, and immediately he found Deng in front of him. He turned, looking for somewhere to pass the ball, but Deng moved even faster.

Right then, TJ thought, I'll go past him. He pushed the ball one side of Deng and raced by him on the other. It was no use. TJ was fast, but Deng was even faster and he beat TJ to the ball, then turned and squeezed a pass to Kelvin, the barrel-shaped Hillside midfielder.

'Stop him, Jamie,' yelled Tulsi.

Jamie tried to move, but he was far too slow. He panted as he ran, and when Kelvin slotted the ball past Rafi into the goal, he groaned and held his stomach. 'Sorry, guys,' he said. 'I've got to rest. Maybe I'll play later.'

'But you haven't done anything!' Tulsi complained.

'Yes, he has,' TJ said. 'He's eaten my dad's lamb and peas.'

'So have you, I bet.'

'Yeah, but I didn't eat as much as Jamie,' TJ laughed, as Jamie flopped onto the bench where Rob was sitting.

They carried on playing, but it was a very one-sided game. Deng was a magician.

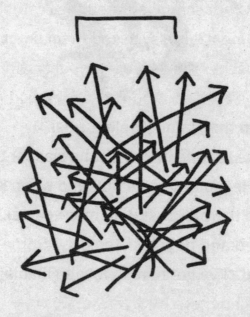

Deng Passes completed 32

Goal assists 17

Hillside 23 Parkview 2
(in the park)

He could win the ball from any of them, and once he had it, it was impossible to get it back from him. And all the time he played his face was split by a banana-shaped grin.

The score finally reached 23–2 and the sun started to go down behind the trees.

'Has your school entered the District Tournament?' Krissy asked them smugly. 'Our teacher thinks we'll probably win.'

'I don't know,' said Tulsi. 'Mr Wood hasn't said anything.'

'Maybe he looked at your defender and decided it wasn't worth entering,' Krissy went on. 'He's getting fatter every day. Look at him now.'

They all looked over at the bench. TJ couldn't believe his eyes. Jamie was unwrapping a chocolate bar. 'What?' Jamie said indignantly when he saw them all watching him. 'I have to keep my strength up, don't I?'

# CHAPTER 2

'You don't think I'm fat, do you?' Jamie asked TJ, as they walked home together. Rob was with them too, deep in thought.

'No,' replied TJ. 'Of course not.'

'I mean, I have to eat. That's what Mum says. I have a healthy appetite.'

'Perhaps you should eat a bit less chocolate,' Rob suggested.

'I'm *not* fat,' Jamie said indignantly.

'No,' said Rob, 'but you have slowed down a bit.'

'I knew it,' muttered Jamie gloomily. 'It's

not fair. Everyone else can eat chocolate. Why can't I?'

'It's not just chocolate,' Rob pointed out. 'You always have two helpings of every-thing.'

'No one's ever moaned before,' Jamie said. 'I was just a bit tired today, that's all. I'll see you on Monday. Maybe Mr Wood will tell us about this tournament.'

TJ and Rob watched Jamie amble off towards his house. 'He needs a proper fitness regime,' Rob said seriously. 'A balanced diet and plenty of exercise. He's

a very important part of the team. If he was properly fit he could be a really good player.'

TJ stopped and stared at Rob. 'You'd better not say all that to Jamie,' he said. 'He'd kill you.'

'Well, someone needs to say it,' replied Rob. 'And they need to say it soon. Jamie's not that unfit yet, but if he doesn't watch out he will be. And then we'll be looking for a new defender.'

On Monday morning, Mr Wood was waiting for them in the classroom wearing a smart suit and a dazzling white shirt with a stripy tie. It was hard to believe he was the same man who wore a faded old T-shirt and jogging bottoms and an old blue baseball cap when he took them for PE and football training.

'I've entered the school team in the District Tournament,' he told them. TJ looked around at his friends and gave them a thumbs-up. Mr Wood saw him. 'I'm warning you all,' he said sternly. 'Nobody's place is safe. Anyone who comes to training every week will have a chance to get in the team.'

TJ glanced over at Jamie, but he didn't seem to be worried. 'OK,' said Mr Wood. 'Now you all know we've had inspectors visiting our school.'

Tulsi pulled a face. The inspectors had been in the school for two whole days the week before. They'd made all the teachers cross and miserable.

'The inspectors will be making visits all this term,' Mr Wood continued. 'And we're going to have to impress them. That's why we're going to do a big project about football.'

Everyone began talking at once. TJ smiled. Mr Wood was really good at finding ways to make everyone work hard.

'We'll be doing lots of exciting things,' Mr Wood explained. 'And we'll make a start by finding out about some footballers. Each of you can pick a name from my hat and use these' – he pointed to a pile of books and newspapers and magazines – 'to write the life story of your player. Find out as much as you can. When they scored their first goal. Who their mums and dads are – and their grandparents, if you like. Some of you can use the Internet too.'

'So it'll be like Literacy and History both at the same time?' asked Jamie.

'You've got it,' smiled Mr Wood. 'It's just the kind of project the inspectors like to see. Especially if you do it really well.'

Rob waved his hand in the air. 'You've forgotten about Numeracy, Mr Wood,' he said. Rob loved statistics. He collected them all the time in his big black notebooks.

Mr Wood laughed. 'I'm sure you'll find a

way to get some stats in your project, Rob,'
he replied. 'Let's get started, everyone.'

'Who have you got?' TJ asked Rob.

'Gary Devlin,' Rob said, looking at his
piece of paper. He closed his eyes and
recited: 'Born 1983 in Leicester. First
appearance—'

'OK, OK,' TJ laughed. 'But you've still got
to write it all down.'

Rob frowned. 'I'll need to check all the
information first,' he said. 'I don't want to
get it wrong.'

After a few minutes TJ looked around the
classroom. Everyone was working hard,
looking through the books and papers and
making notes. 'I don't get it,' TJ whispered
to Rob. 'When we have to write stories you
hardly write anything, but now you're
doing all this. You've written more than
anyone.'

'I hate stuff that's made up,' Rob

explained. 'Last year our teacher made us write stories all the time. I hated it. So they started making me have special help from Miss Berry.'

'But everyone likes stories.'

'Well, I don't,' said Rob. 'Stories aren't true. I like facts.'

'Get on with your work,' Mr Wood snapped, 'or you can both stay in at break.'

Rob grinned at TJ. Mr Wood was very strict in class, but they both knew that he was a great teacher. And, just as important, he was a brilliant football coach.

At lunch time Jamie, TJ and Tulsi waited patiently in the queue in the dinner hall. The children nearby were all eating packed lunches. 'It's worse than the zoo,' TJ said to Jamie, as they watched the little kids in Class One throwing sandwiches at each other. Janice, the head dinner lady, was trying to stop them, but they just ignored her.

Jamie wasn't interested in the little kids. 'Yes!' he exclaimed, as they reached the hatch. 'It's shepherd's pie! My favourite!'

'Hello, Jamie love,' said Mrs Hubbard, the school cook. She was wearing a red-and-white striped apron and her enormous shape seemed to fill the whole hatch. 'You love my shepherd's pie, don't you? I'll give you a little bit extra. And would you like some chips with it?'

'Yes, please,' said Jamie. 'And a bit of sweetcorn too.'

'There,' said Mrs Hubbard, handing Jamie a plateful of food that was piled up like a mountain range. 'Oh, wait a second, love. You should have some salad. We have to be healthy, you know.' She balanced a small piece of lettuce on top of the mountain.

'Good boy,' she said. 'And it's toffee crunch for afters, so I'll save you a nice sticky bit.'

'Please don't give him so much food, Mrs Hubbard,' said Tulsi, as Jamie wandered off to find a seat. 'He's getting really unfit.'

'Nonsense, dear,' Mrs Hubbard replied. 'He's a growing lad. And he loves my cooking. It does me a power of good to see a boy with a healthy appetite.'

'We have to do something,' TJ said to Tulsi. 'He's our friend, and if he doesn't watch out, he'll be so unfit that Mr Wood will drop him from the team.'

# CHAPTER 3

Training was on Wednesday afternoon.
As they changed in the classroom, TJ saw
Jamie take a plastic box from his bag. 'I
don't believe it,' he said to Rafi, who was
chatting to his friend, Ariyan. 'Look at Jamie!'

Jamie opened the box, took out a
sandwich and began to munch. 'What are
you doing?' TJ said. 'We're supposed to be
playing football, not having a picnic.'

'Mum thought I'd need the energy,' Jamie
said, although it was hard to make out what

he was saying through his enormous mouthful of sandwich.

'I give up,' TJ said. 'Anyone would think you didn't want to play, Jamie.'

TJ looked across the room and saw Danny watching them. Danny was a good foot-baller, and he'd been the goalkeeper for their match against Hillside, but none of TJ's friends liked him. TJ had the feeling that Danny would be pleased if Jamie lost his place in the team.

Outside on the field Mr Wood and Miss Berry had marked out a grid of ten-metre squares using plastic cones. 'It looks as if everyone in Year Six is here,' said Mr Wood. 'So Miss Berry is going to help out at every session from now on.'

They all jogged round the field a few times to warm up, and TJ could see that Jamie was struggling badly.

'OK, everyone,' Mr Wood said. 'Line up

along the edge of the grid there. I want you to sprint to the next row of cones, touch the ground, then sprint back again. After that, sprint to the next row, touch, and sprint back. OK? On my whistle. Go!'

There was no time for TJ to worry about Jamie any more. He sprinted, turned and ran. Just as he thought he was getting his breath back, the whistle blew and they were

off again. Soon TJ's shirt was wet with sweat, and his lungs were bursting.

'That's good,' said Mr Wood. 'Now get one ball between two and work in one of the squares. Control the ball, pass it, and move to a new position. See if you can pass the ball to where you think your partner is going to be. Go.'

'All right, Jamie?' TJ said.

Jamie couldn't answer. He was puffing and very red in the face. TJ collected a ball and Jamie followed him to a square.

'Listen,' Jamie said. 'You run around and I'll stay here, OK? In the middle. It'll look as if I'm doing something.'

'It won't work,' said TJ. 'But we can try it if you like.'

So TJ ran around the edge of the square, and Jamie sprayed passes to him. Jamie's passes weren't all that accurate, so TJ had plenty of running to do before Mr Wood blew his whistle again.

'Right, everyone,' he said, as a tall figure in a woolly hat walked across the playground towards them. 'I expect you think I'm trying to torture you!' There was a chorus of groans. Even TJ could feel the tiredness in his muscles. 'I'm making you work hard for a very good reason,' Mr Wood continued. 'When we play in this tournament we'll have to play at least three matches. Then if we win our group, we'll have to play another three to win the tournament. And we may find ourselves playing extra time too. So you're going to have to be extremely fit – all of you. Because we want to win, don't we?' There was a ragged cheer.

'OK, then. Now we're going to play a little game. Two v two in a square. You can have two touches, one to control the ball and one to pass. Each pair has to try and keep the ball. Both teams start with ten points. If the ball runs out of the square then the team that touched it last loses a point. TJ, you can play with Marshall against me and Rodrigo.'

TJ felt a jolt of excitement. He hadn't noticed Marshall arriving. Marshall Jones played for Wanderers in the Premier League. He was an old friend of Mr Wood, and without Marshall's help TJ was pretty sure that they wouldn't be playing any football at Parkview School.

But this was the first time Marshall had ever joined in a training session, and TJ couldn't believe that he was actually going to play with him. He glanced across to see how Jamie was getting on, and saw Mr Wood talking to him.

'I've got an important job for you, Jamie,' Mr Wood was saying. 'Leila, Diane and Ebony have never played before, and they need some help from an expert, so I'd like you to work with them. Is that OK?'

Jamie tried to look pleased. 'Of course,' he said. 'I'll do my best.'

TJ caught Rafi's eye. They both knew Mr Wood was being kind to Jamie. He could have just told him he wasn't fit enough to carry on.

Marshall shook hands with TJ. 'Let's show these guys how it's done,' he said, as they waited for Mr Wood to sort out the other groups. 'Looks like your friend Jamie's put on a few pounds, yeah? You need to get him fit.'

'I know,' said TJ. 'But it's not that easy.'

# CHAPTER 4

They began to play. TJ suddenly
remembered that he'd seen this game
before when Marshall had taken them to see
Wanderers play City. The Wanderers team
had used the game as a warm-up, and now
he was playing it with an actual Wanderers
player. 'Hey, come on, TJ, wake up,' Marshall
said, as the ball ran past his foot. 'That's a
point we've lost.'

Rodrigo retrieved the ball and passed to
Mr Wood. Pass . . . pass . . . pass . . . It was
impossible to get the ball off them. Then

suddenly TJ saw Mr Wood's eyes flick to the left and he stretched out a foot to intercept the pass. He heard Marshall's shout, back-heeled the ball and darted off to find more space. The ball came back to him hard and fast. There was no time to think. His instincts took over. All the hours and days of practising against the wall in his back garden now paid off. He took the pace off the ball with the inside of his foot, and at the same time he was moving away from Mr Wood, making himself half a metre of space to play the ball back to Marshall.

Faster and faster, TJ and Marshall moved the ball around the square. Finally Mr Wood stopped. He was out of breath, and he winced slightly as he put weight on one of his legs.

'Hey, man, are you OK?' said Marshall. 'I didn't know it was going to turn into a full-scale workout. TJ, that was incredible!'

TJ couldn't say a thing. Now that they had stopped, his legs felt like jelly.

Mr Wood blew his whistle and gathered everyone together. 'Well done, everyone. Now, Marshall didn't just come here to give me a hard time on the football pitch,' he said. 'We've arranged for all of Year Six to go on an official school trip to the Wanderers training ground this Friday as part of our football project.'

He waited until the excited chatter died down, and then he continued. 'We'll watch Wanderers train and then we're all going to do a fitness test.'

'Awesome,' breathed Rob. 'We'll have so many stats. Will they test everyone's heart rate too?'

'I don't know,' laughed Mr Wood. 'I'm sure we can see all the equipment they use though, right, Marshall? We'll learn a lot about Sports Science for our project. We'll find out how footballers keep fit and healthy – what kind of exercise they do and what they eat. The inspectors will love it.'

As they walked home, Jamie was lost in gloomy thoughts. 'Come on, Jamie,' said Tulsi. 'We're going to see Wanderers. So we'll get to meet them all, which will be amazing.'

'And have our fitness tested. I'm going to look stupid. I don't want to come.'

But when Friday arrived Jamie was looking more cheerful. 'I've been dieting,' he said in the playground before school. 'I reckon it's made a difference.'

'Great!' TJ replied. 'What have you done?'

'Well, this morning I had a really small breakfast,' Jamie said proudly. 'I just had one bowl of cereal and a couple of slices of toast . . .'

'Excellent!' exclaimed Tulsi.

'And then Mum made me bacon and eggs,' Jamie continued. 'But I only had one egg, and I didn't have a sausage . . .'

'Oh,' Tulsi said.

'And then a couple of bananas, because they're fruit, aren't they? And you have to eat fruit.'

'Hmmm,' said Rob. 'I estimate you had about fifteen hundred calories for breakfast. Are you planning to eat many more meals today?'

'Just my packed lunch,' Jamie said. 'And my tea when I get home. And maybe a little snack before I go to bed.'

'But what will you have for tea?' Rob asked him.

'Pie and chips, probably,' Jamie said. 'And my mum makes really nice afters. Sponge pudding and custard maybe. Mmmmm.' He licked his lips.

Rob frowned. 'Well, if all your meals are as big as that,' he said, 'you'll probably have to run about fifteen kilometres just to get rid of your extra calories.'

Jamie stared at him. 'Are you sure?' he said. 'That can't be right.'

'You're just going to have to eat less, Jamie,' laughed Tulsi. 'Or eat different things.'

'Or play lots of football,' said Jamie with a grin. 'Come on, we can play for ten minutes before school.'

The journey to the Wanderers training ground was short. The coach pulled up in front of a brick building with WANDERERS FC in big letters across the front. They all climbed out and a young man in a tracksuit greeted them.

'I'm Phil,' he said. 'I'm a coach with the Academy here at Wanderers. Do you all know about the Academy?' Most of the class shook their heads. 'It's where we coach the very best young players,' Phil told them. 'You can start when you're eight years old.'

'But how do you join?' asked Rafi.

'*We* find *you*,' said Phil with a smile. 'We have scouts everywhere watching matches. School matches, Sunday League matches. We're always looking for talent. If we see someone we like we usually invite them to our Player Development Centre so we can help them to improve. And then, maybe, we ask them to join the Academy. Anyway, Marshall asked me to show you around today. I guess you'd like to watch the first team training, yeah?'

Phil led them along a pathway and through a car park full of shiny black four-wheel drives and sports cars. 'There's Marshall's Ferrari,' said Rob.

Phil laughed. 'He loves that car,' he said. 'Look! Here we are.'

They turned a corner by a huge white building and saw green football pitches stretching into the distance. Close by, footballers were dribbling balls backwards and forwards between rows of cones at incredible speed. 'It's the same as what Mr Wood makes us do,' said TJ, surprised.

'It's still football, isn't it?' said Phil. 'We all play the same game, so we all have to practise the same things, no matter how good we are.'

They watched the Wanderers players go through a whole series of drills, and then the players split into two groups. 'The strikers and midfield players are going to practise shooting,' Phil told them. 'And the defenders are practising heading.'

They watched as the defenders took turns to kick high balls to each other. 'That must really hurt,' said Jamie, as one of them headed a ball that came down from an enormous height.

'That's their job,' Phil told him. 'A

defender has to head it clear. If he waits for it to drop in front of him, an attacker will have a much better chance of winning the ball.'

'I'd rather do *that*,' said Tulsi, pointing to the other end of the pitch. The players were working in teams of three, passing the ball between them like lightning until one player ended with a shot on goal.

'Well,' Phil said, 'they'll be taking a break in a moment. How about you try it for yourselves?'

# CHAPTER 5

Marshall came over to talk to them, as the players left the pitch. 'They're going to have a go at that drill,' Phil told him.

'Well, you watch out for TJ here. He's got a shot that can knock over a head teacher from twenty-five metres! Good luck, all of you. I'll see you in a while.'

'Is that true?' Phil asked TJ.

'It was an accident,' TJ said with a grin.

'Well, you be careful. I don't want to get hurt.'

The drill was more complicated than

anything they'd done at school. Mr Wood helped Phil to get them organized. TJ was working with Rodrigo and Tommy. He hit the ball to Tommy on the wing. Tommy pretended to run away from him, but then turned back and hit the ball first time with the outside of his foot. It curved in towards Rodrigo, who was standing on the edge of the penalty area. Rodrigo's job was simply to lay the ball back to Tommy, who followed after his own pass and shot at the goal.

'Great stuff,' said Phil. 'Did you under-stand that, everyone? Now, this time you change places. TJ goes on the wing, Tommy lays it back, and Rodrigo joins the queue. Easy, isn't it?'

'I don't get it,' wailed Leila. 'I can't even kick it that far.'

'I bet you can,' said Jamie. He'd taken his job of helping the girls very seriously. 'Just do what I showed you the other day.

You'll be fine.'

TJ smiled. That was why Jamie was such an important part of the team. He was always helping people. Very soon they were all working smoothly, taking turns and then running back to join the line, and even Rob had put down his notebook for once and was joining in. 'Well done, everyone,' said Phil. 'Let's make it more interesting now. You've been shooting into an empty net, but now I'm going to go in goal. We'll see if you can beat me.'

As TJ moved slowly forward in the line, Phil saved shot after shot. 'Come on,' he said, laughing. 'You can do better than that. Where's the lad who knocked the head teacher over?'

TJ was at the front now. He played the ball to Tommy, who curled a great pass to Rodrigo. TJ was certain Tommy was going to score, as Rodrigo set the ball up for him nicely, but Tommy's left-foot shot crashed against the foot of the post. 'Great try!' said Phil. 'That's twelve nil to me.'

Jamie was right behind TJ in the line. 'Go on, TJ,' he said. 'Blast it! He's just laughing at us.'

TJ ran out to the wing and Jamie hit the ball to him. TJ flicked the ball to Tommy and raced after the pass. Tommy stunned the ball neatly into his path and TJ put every-thing he had into a low drive towards the far post. It hit the back of the net before Phil could even move. He stood there staring at

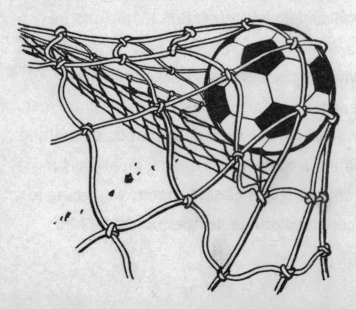

TJ, as he exchanged high-fives with Tommy.

'What did I tell you?' Marshall said. He'd been watching from the side with Mr Wood and the Wanderers first-team coach. 'You're lucky you didn't get in the way of that one, Phil. Nice one, TJ! I couldn't have hit that better myself.'

'You're doing a great job with these kids, Johnny,' the first-team coach said to Mr Wood, with a quick glance at TJ. 'It looks like you've got some real talent there. But we have to get on now. I'll see you later.'

For nearly an hour the kids from Parkview watched the Wanderers team training.

'Dexter Gordon smiled at me,' said Tulsi, with a dreamy expression on her face.

'Yes, well, now you've all had a good rest,' Mr Wood said, 'we're going to do something called a beep test.'

'What's that?' asked Jamie.

'It'll tell us exactly how fit you all are,'

replied Mr Wood. 'And then we can plan how to get fitter. It's easy. All you have to do is run between those sets of cones. You time your runs to match the beeps, and after a while the beeps will start getting faster. When you can't keep up, then you stop and we give you your score. Off you go!'

TJ soon found himself running comfortably in time to the beeps, and so did a lot of the others. But as the beeps began to speed up, people started drop out. Jamie was dragging his feet. He was falling behind. 'You can do it, Jamie,' said TJ. 'Keep going. Breathe!'

But it was no use. Two more beeps and TJ heard Mr Wood saying, 'You're out, Jamie. Come and sit down.'

TJ turned with the beep and saw Jamie bent double, gasping for breath. Next time he turned, the beeps had speeded up again and he was starting to breathe a little faster himself. More and more kids dropped out, until only TJ and Tulsi were left running. TJ glanced across at Tulsi. She hardly seemed to be making any effort. TJ's legs were beginning to feel like lumps of wood. At the next turn he was late, and Mr Wood yelled, 'Come on, TJ, you have to catch up.'

He pushed his legs as fast as they would go, and at the next turn he was exactly in time with the beep, but now he saw that Tulsi was running away from him. He kept telling his legs to move, but they wouldn't. It was like running through treacle.

'That's enough, TJ,' Mr Wood told him. TJ collapsed on the ground, as Tulsi carried on, run- ning, turning,

faster and faster. And at each turn, everyone cheered.

Finally Tulsi was forced to stop. 'Great work, Tulsi,' Mr Wood said, as they all walked back to the bus.

'How did you do that?' TJ said. 'I thought I was faster than you.'

'You are faster,' Tulsi said with a grin. 'But you can't keep going as long. Statistics don't lie, do they, Rob?'

'You are officially the fittest in Year Six,' Rob said.

'And we all know who's unfit,' said Danny spitefully.

Jamie just walked on ahead of them. TJ hoped he hadn't heard. He knew that Jamie really was doing his best. He just needed a little help, that was all.

# CHAPTER 6

'We have to *do* something,' Tulsi said after
school. They were standing in the playground – Tommy, Rodrigo, Rafi, Tulsi, Rob
and TJ. Jamie had walked off without saying
a word.

'It's not just that he eats too much,' Rafi
said. 'It's *what* he eats. All those potatoes
and chips and pies.'

'And puddings,' said Tulsi. 'Don't forget
the puddings. I've been round to Jamie's
house. They always have afters. Steamed

puddings with custard and banoffee pie and—'

'Don't,' interrupted TJ. 'You're making me hungry.'

'Just imagine what it must be like for Jamie,' Tulsi said. 'And then when he gets to school there's Mrs Hubbard piling his plate up so high he can hardly carry it.'

'So, come on then,' said Tommy. 'You're so clever. You think of something.'

'Yeah, what do *you* eat that makes you so fit?' asked TJ.

'We eat vegetables mostly. And rice and beans. And fruit. My mum's a really good cook. We don't ever have chips.'

'Fish,' said Rodrigo. 'I eat fish.'

'Hey, Rodrigo!' TJ said. 'Brilliant English.'

Rodrigo smiled. 'Fish good,' he said, and he licked his lips then smacked them together, making them all laugh.

'You know what?' Tulsi said. 'We all eat

different kinds of food. Maybe if we gave Jamie some recipes . . .'

'It's Jamie's mum who needs the recipes,' said TJ.

'Yeah, and Mrs Hubbard,' agreed Rafi. 'Just imagine if she cooked nice curries, and rice . . .'

'And chapattis,' said Tulsi.

'Fish!' said Rodrigo triumphantly.

'And pasta with tomato sauce,' said Tommy. 'My dad taught *me* to cook it so Mrs Hubbard could do it easily.'

'It'll never happen,' Tulsi said, shaking her head. 'Mrs Hubbard has been cooking the same things as long as I can remember, and I bet Jamie's mum has too. Unless . . .'

'What?'

'Maybe we could have a day at school. A food day. No, a *world* food day. I bet my mum and dad would make something for it.'

'Like they did when we fixed the pitch,' said Rafi. 'It was brilliant.'

'My dad could make lamb and peas,' TJ said, then his face fell. 'But Jamie ate double helpings of that. He stuffed himself. It's not going to work. He'll just eat more.'

'No,' said Tulsi. 'It'll work. He didn't do himself anything like as much damage filling himself with lamb and peas as he does with sticky toffee pudding. We'll show everyone there's loads of nice things you can eat that don't make you fat.'

'We could have football too,' said Rob, who had been thinking hard. 'A mini World Cup, food, football, fitness and fun. How about that?'

'Genius,' said TJ. 'I mean, it can be part of our football project, can't it? The World Cup will be Geography and we'll be doing Food Technology too.'

'And there's lots of science,' added Rob.

'I bet Mr Wood will love it. Let's go and ask him.'

*

Rob was right. Mr Wood *did* love the idea, and so did their head teacher, Mr Burrows. 'Just the thing!' he said when Mr Wood took them to see him. 'You go ahead and organize it, Mr Wood.'

TJ's dad was excited too, when TJ told him about it that evening. 'I've been thinking, though, Dad,' TJ said. 'It's going to take more than a World Food Day to get Jamie fit.'

'It sounds like *you* need to be fitter too,' his mum told him with a smile. 'I'm very impressed that Tulsi beat you in that beep test.'

'And Dad could lose a bit of weight as well,' laughed Joey.

'Says who?' Mr Wilson looked down at his stomach. Then he shook his head and laughed. 'I suppose you've got a point,' he said. 'Listen, I'll tell you what we'll do. Why don't we all go running together in the evenings? The Wilson family and any of TJ's friends who want to come. Especially Jamie. He's a great lad, and it would be a shame if he wasn't in the team.'

'Not me,' said Lou. 'I'm fit. I go dancing.'

'Me neither,' laughed TJ's mum. 'I've got my swimming. But I'm looking forward to seeing this!'

The next day Mr Wood put Year Six to work, organizing the day.

'It'll be on a Saturday,' he said. 'We have just three weeks. We'll ask mums and dads to make food, and every class is going to have a stall. You lot are going to make a big display about how to get fit and healthy. We can use the information we collected on our visit to Wanderers. Rob, I want you to organize the World Cup tournament. We're doing it for fun, so teams can have players of any age in them. For instance, Rafi could play with his mum and dad and his little sisters.'

Everyone started laughing and talking. Mr Wood held up a hand.

'You can choose which country you'd like to be,' he said. 'But if there's more than one entry for that country then it'll be first come, first served.'

Rob was already writing in his notebook.

'Is that OK, Rob?' Mr Wood asked.

'I'm on it,' Rob replied.

TJ looked at him. Rob seemed to be getting more confident with every day that passed. But there was no time to think about that. Suddenly there was a huge amount of work to do.

'Come on, Jamie,' TJ said. 'You're really good at designing posters. We can have plates of steaming food, and mad football pictures.'

'I can't,' Jamie said. 'I don't even want to think about food. I'm starving.'

'No way,' said TJ. 'You're never starving.'

'Well, I am today,' Jamie said. 'I had corn-flakes for breakfast.'

'So? That's what I had.'

'You don't understand. That's *all* I had. If this is what it takes to get fit, I don't think I want to play football. You all thought up this crazy idea just to torment me, didn't you?'

'It'll be fun,' TJ laughed. 'And you don't have to starve yourself. Just give up the sticky toffee pudding. And there's another thing . . .' TJ told him about his dad's idea.

'We won't go far,' he said. 'Dad reckons one or maybe two kilometres at first.' He turned to the others. 'You can all come if you want,' he said.

'I'm fit already,' laughed Tulsi.

'I'll come,' Rob said. 'If you're sure it's all right.'

'Of course it is,' TJ told him. 'We're going to the Sports Centre on London Road. They've got a floodlit running trail. How about you, Jamie?'

'I don't know,' said Jamie gloomily. 'Right now, I'm weak with hunger. I might not even have the strength to walk home.'

# CHAPTER 7

Three weeks passed. The whole school buzzed with excitement, and the smells of cooking filled every corner. 'I can't stand it,' Jamie said. 'I'm going to go crazy with hunger. Look at me, my mouth is watering.'

'We're doing this for you, Jamie,' Tulsi told him. 'So stop grumbling. Are you ready for training tonight?'

'I'm wasting away,' Jamie said. 'I've hardly eaten a thing for weeks. And I think all the running is wearing my legs out. I'm sure they're getting shorter.'

TJ laughed. Jamie had been running three

times a week with him and his dad and Rob. The first two times they'd just jogged along really slowly, but since then they'd definitely speeded up a little and last night Jamie had hardly complained at all.

That afternoon at training Mr Wood had news for them. 'I've arranged a friendly match for us,' he said. 'To help us prepare for the tournament.'

'Not Hillside again,' said Rafi.

'No,' said Mr Wood. 'It's against a Sunday League team called Meadow Green Wasps.'

'Sad name,' Tommy said. 'We'll beat them easily.'

'I doubt it,' said Rob, consulting his note-book. 'Wasps won the Sunday League last year. They never lost a match.'

'Exactly,' said Mr Wood. 'So we'd better do some work.'

'You see?' TJ said to Jamie, as they practised dribbling and sprinting. 'You

## Sunday League
## Under 10s
## Meadow Green Wasps record

Played 20

Won 18

Drawn 2

Goals for 63

Goals against 12

Captain = Leroy (35 goals)

really are getting fitter.'

'I don't *feel* fitter,' Jamie said.

'Yeah, but you're keeping up. Not like last time.'

Jamie paused. 'Look,' he said. 'Rob's joining in.'

'Hey, that's great,' TJ said. Rob was dribbling very carefully in and out of the cones, his head bent in concentration. Then TJ heard Danny's voice.

'Look at him! You should stick to your notebook, Rob.'

Mr Wood turned sharply. 'Danny,' he said. 'Over here. The rest of you, carry on.'

No one heard what Mr Wood said to Danny in a low voice, but they could see how angry he was. Danny walked back to his place with a very red face.

'Well done, everyone,' Mr Wood said at the end of the session. 'You've all worked really hard, and now I'm going to tell you who's in the squad to play Wasps. It's seven-a-side and we'll have two subs. Tommy, Ariyan, Rafi, Rodrigo, Danny, Cameron, Tulsi, TJ . . .' He paused. There was just one place left now. 'Leila, I know you've only just started, but you've learned really fast. And you're very fit, so I'm going to give you a chance.'

Leila shrieked and clapped her hands. While her friends congratulated her, Mr Wood took Jamie to one side. 'I'm sorry, Jamie,' he said. 'I just don't think you'd make it through a match at the moment.'

'Leila couldn't even kick a ball until I showed her,' grumbled Jamie later. 'What's the point in starving myself if I still don't get in the team?'

'I keep telling you,' Tulsi said. 'You don't have to starve. You just have to eat different food. You'll see on Saturday. Have you got a team for the World Cup?'

Jamie brightened up. 'Yeah,' he said. 'The Carter boys. We're going to be Iceland. Me and my four brothers.'

'What, even little Max?' said TJ. Max was only four and he hadn't even started school yet.

'Yeah,' laughed Jamie. 'He's good, you

know. When he kicks you, you really feel it!'

*

On Saturday morning TJ woke up early and pulled back the curtains. It was a sunny day with just a few fluffy clouds. The leaves were starting to fall from the trees, but there was still a bit of summer in the air. When they arrived at the school Mr Wood and Miss Berry were fastening a banner above the gate:

# PARKVIEW WORLD CUP

And Mr Coggins the caretaker was tying other banners onto the fence:

# FUN! FOOD! FITNESS! FOOTBALL!

Teachers and children were carrying tables out of the school and setting up stalls. 'We were going to have the stalls inside,' Miss Berry said, 'but it's such a lovely day that we decided to bring everything out here.'

'I'm not sure about the bread rolls the Reception children have made,' TJ said, laughing. 'They're really weird shapes!'

'They smell good though,' said Jamie. 'And look at all those other stalls.'

It wasn't just TJ's mum and dad who'd been cooking. Tulsi's parents had made lots of delicious Indian vegetarian food.

Rodrigo's mum and dad were standing, smiling, behind a tempting collection of fish dishes from Portugal. There was Moroccan food and Spanish food and Polish food and Chinese food, and it all looked mouth-wateringly good.

Jamie had his whole family with him. His dad was a giant in jeans and a leather jacket with a fat gold earring and Jamie's infectious grin. 'I would have done a stall myself,'

Jamie's mum said. 'But healthy food isn't my strong point. And anyway, my boys like burgers and chips.'

'We like other things too,' Jamie said. 'Come on, Mum. Let's try out the food.'

'Iceland aren't going to win the World Cup,' said Rafi. 'Jamie won't be able to move by this afternoon.'

'It's Jamaica who will win,' said TJ's dad. 'Represented by the Wilson family.'

'Jamaica's where my grandma and grandpa were born,' TJ explained.

'Look,' said Tulsi, suddenly pointing. 'What do they want?'

Two men in grey suits were walking in through the school gates. TJ recognized them at once. 'It's the inspectors,' he said.

'Mr Burrows must have asked them to come,' said Mr Wood, who was standing nearby. 'We'd better make sure they have a good time.'

# CHAPTER 8

'TJ,' said Mr Wood. 'This is Mr Grayson and Mr Turvey. Will you show them around? Maybe Tulsi could go with you?'

'Er, yes. OK, Mr Wood,' said TJ. 'Where would you like to go?' he asked the inspectors.

'Let's look at the stalls the children have set up,' said Mr Turvey. From a distance the two inspectors had looked like twins, but now TJ could see the difference. Mr Turvey was gazing around with interest, but Mr Grayson looked as though he had just smelled something nasty.

'This is a good school really,' Tulsi said. 'Everyone's been working very hard.'

'I'm glad you think so,' Mr Turvey said. 'But you know, we have to look at the facts. We can't just take your word for it.'

'You sound like Rob,' TJ said. 'He only believes in facts.'

'This is Year Five,' Tulsi said. Year Five had been making fruit salad and the colours on the stall were dazzling.

'Would you like to try some, sir?' asked the girl behind the stall.

'Thanks,' said Mr Turvey. 'How about this one?'

'That's mango, guava, pineapple and coconut,' said the girl. 'It's tropical. Would you like the recipe?'

She handed Mr Turvey a piece of paper. It was covered with beautifully neat hand-writing and pictures of fruit.

Mr Turvey showed it to Mr Grayson, who

sniffed. 'Who wrote this?' he enquired drily.

'Me,' said the girl. 'Loretta, see?' She pointed to her name on the bottom of the sheet.

'Remarkable,' said Mr Grayson. 'We've never seen work of this quality here before. Are you sure this wasn't written by your parents, young lady?'

A small crowd of interested mums and dads had gathered around the inspectors, and there was a sudden commotion at the back. A large West Indian lady pushed her way to the front. 'Excuse me,' she said. 'Are you calling my daughter a liar?'

Mr Grayson took a step back. 'No, madam. Of course not. But the inspection of a school is a serious matter. We don't want to make any mistakes.'

'I should think not,' said Loretta's mum. 'It would be a very big mistake to say anything bad about this school, I can tell you. Look at all the wonderful things they have done here today. Shame on you.'

There was a cheer from the crowd. TJ and Tulsi led the inspectors on to look at the other stalls. 'That told you, eh, Charles?' said Mr Turvey, and TJ thought he saw just the hint of a smile on his face.

But Mr Grayson frowned even harder, as they went from stall to stall and saw that every class had produced posters and recipes and even little booklets. 'It's like a different school from the one we visited last term,' he said suspiciously. 'Something fishy is going on here.'

'No,' Tulsi said with a grin. 'You can just smell Rodrigo's stall, that's all.' She pointed at the bowls of fishy food. TJ kicked her. He had the feeling that Mr Grayson didn't have a sense of humour.

'Let's take a look at the football,' Mr Turvey said. 'I see you have a pupil organizing it all.'

'This is Rob,' TJ said. 'The one who likes facts. He's in charge.'

Rob had drawn out a complicated plan to show who was playing who, and which of the three small pitches they were playing on.

'We have to have three pitches,' he explained. 'Otherwise we'll never get all the matches played. But that's OK. Mini-pitches for a mini-World Cup. We're having mini-matches too, only two minutes each way.'

'This is incredible,' Mr Turvey said, studying Rob's plan. 'You've done a complete timetable!'

'Are you planning to enter a team?' Rob asked him. 'I can let you have time to think about it.' He looked at his watch. 'You have an hour and twenty-three minutes before the first match. That's so people can recover from all the eating,' he added.

For the first time, Mr Turvey's face broke into a smile. 'I don't think so,' he said. 'I'm afraid my footballing days are over.'

'Mr Coggins is playing,' Rob said. 'I'm sure he's a lot older than you are. He's in the dinner ladies' team. They're Mexico.'

TJ made his way back to his mum and dad's stall, where he saw a familiar tall figure in a woolly hat tucking into a bowl of his dad's lamb and peas. 'Hi, Marshall,' he said. 'You're not going to play, are you?'

'No way! We've got a game tomorrow. Imagine if I got injured again! I'll tell you what though – why don't I ref some matches? I don't mind doing that.'

'And you have to officially open the World Cup,' Tulsi said. 'Please?'

'Well, OK,' laughed Marshall. 'But first I want to eat some more of this food. Where did you get this recipe? It's fantastic. Just like my granny used to make in Jamaica.'

'I got it from *my* granny,' laughed Mr Wilson. 'Hey, maybe my granny knew your granny!'

TJ left them eating and laughing. Everyone seemed to be having a great time. He spotted Mrs Hubbard, the school cook, standing at Tulsi's stall. 'I don't like spicy food,' she was saying, wrinkling her nose. 'Never have.'

'Why don't you try some of this aubergine?' Tulsi's mum said.

'Oh, no. I couldn't. I don't like those overjean thingies.'

'I bet you've never even tried one,' Jamie said. 'They're great. Everything Mrs Patel's made is great. I've tried it all!'

'Jamie!' said TJ. 'You're trying to stay fit.'

'It's OK,' Jamie said. 'I'm having a day

off. I'll start again tomorrow. Go on, Mrs Hubbard. Try some.'

Mrs Hubbard took the little bowl from Mrs Patel and sniffed it suspiciously. 'Hmm,' she said. 'It doesn't smell too bad, I suppose.'

She put some in her mouth. Very slowly, her face changed. 'Oh,' she said. 'Ah!' Then she took another mouthful, and another. 'Well,' she said finally. 'That was *delicious*. Who would have thought it?'

'You should try absolutely everything,' Jamie said. 'I'll tell you what, I'll help you, Mrs H. There's lots of other good stalls.'

TJ and Tulsi watched them walk away.

'He's getting fatter by the second,' said Tulsi. 'And after all the hard work he's done. If I hadn't thought of the World Food Day, this would never have happened.'

# CHAPTER 9

'Ladies and gentlemen, boys and girls,' Marshall announced. 'I now declare the Parkview World Cup well and truly open.'

All the food had been eaten and everyone had moved onto the field to watch the matches – and to play. The biggest crowd was waiting for the game on Pitch 3 – Mexico v India. 'Come on,' TJ said to the rest of his family, 'we have to see this.'

Tulsi's team included her mum and dad, and her little brother, Sunil, who was in Year Two. And in goal, grinning broadly, was a very small lady in a bright green tracksuit.

'My gran,' Tulsi told them proudly. 'She only just arrived. She's come all the way from Birmingham to play.' She waved to her gran and her gran waved back, bouncing up and down on the spot.

The other team had Mr Coggins playing as striker. The dinner ladies all wore matching pink tracksuits. 'From our keep-fit club,' Janice told them. 'We brought one for Mr C, but he won't wear it for some reason.'

Mr Coggins was doing complicated warm-ups in the centre of the tiny pitch. He was wearing an ancient Wanderers shirt and a pair of baggy shorts. 'I hope he's not going to do himself an injury,' Janice said, laughing, and then Rob sounded a horn, and the matches kicked off on all three pitches at the same time.

Mexico never had a chance. Tulsi's dad passed to her and she dribbled past Janice, stopped on the edge of the penalty area and passed to Sunil, who shot neatly into the corner.

'Did you see that?' Rafi said, tapping TJ on the shoulder. 'Tulsi passed when she could have scored!'

'Incredible,' agreed TJ. 'Hey, look. Mr Coggins is on a run!'

The caretaker was approaching the goal. Tulsi's mum stood in his way, but Mr Coggins did something very clever with his body, pretending to go one way, and then slipping easily past Mrs Patel. Only Tulsi's gran stood in his way. He sent his shot towards the corner, but Tulsi's gran surprised everyone by diving gracefully and plucking the ball out of the air. She rolled twice, stood up and then bowled the ball right down the middle of the pitch to Tulsi's feet. Tulsi had no trouble scoring.

India won the match 4–0. 'Your gran is amazing,' TJ said. 'How did she do that?'

'Tae kwon do,' said Tulsi's gran. 'It keeps you flexible, young man.'

'Hey, TJ,' said his dad. 'Stop jabbering. We're on next. Jamaica v Brazil.'

Jamaica defeated Brazil 6–0. TJ's dad was over the moon. 'Amazing,' he said afterwards. 'It's the first time Jamaica has ever beaten Brazil! We were brilliant.'

'Hey, Dad,' said Joey. 'They're in Year One! How could we not beat them? They're only six years old.'

'We still had to win the match,' Mr Wilson said. 'My goal was genius!'

Jamaica defeated Australia next, and then they were in the semifinal. 'Who are we playing next?' asked Lou. 'If we can win, maybe we can go on to win the World Cup.'

'It's Iceland,' TJ said. 'Jamie's team.'

'Matt's team, you mean. We've got to win, TJ, you hear me? I'll never hear the end of it if we lose.'

'All right,' said TJ. 'Calm down. It's only a game, Lou. I mean, it's not even real football.'

'Don't be stupid, TJ,' Lou told him, with a grim look on her face. 'We simply *have* to win.'

The cones that had marked out the small pitches had been removed and the teams were going to play the semifinals on the bigger pitch they normally used. TJ was surprised to see that the two inspectors were still there, talking to the excited crowd of mums and dads and grandparents and friends.

'OK,' said Marshall, who was refereeing the game. 'We're playing five minutes each way. No extra time. Just penalties if it's a draw.'

'Hey, Jamie?' said TJ. 'What are you doing?'

'What does it look like?' Jamie said. 'I'm

going in goal. I'm too full to move.'

'World Cup Final, here we come,' said Mr Wilson, as he kicked off to TJ. 'They've lost their defender. We'll beat them easily.'

But little Max had other ideas. He nicked the ball from TJ's dad's feet and passed to Matt. Lou charged at him, and Matt took a step back, raising his arms in the air.

'Thanks, Matt,' said Lou, kicking the ball forward towards TJ. 'Go on, TJ. Shoot!'

TJ looked up. It was weird. Jamie seemed to fill the goal. TJ had never realized before how long his arms and legs were, and they were only small goals. He made up his mind, and blasted the ball.

Jamie reached out both hands and grabbed it. Then a grin split his face. 'You never thought I'd do that, did you?' he said, and he threw the ball out to Matt. Lou barged straight into him, knocking him to one side.

'Ref!' yelled Matt. 'It's not fair.'

Marshall grinned. 'Nothing in it,' he said. 'It was a fifty-fifty ball. Play on.'

Lou pulled a face at Matt and passed the ball to her dad.

'Hey, now you'll see something,' Mr Wilson said. 'I'll show you my famous move!'

The Jamaica team all groaned. Mrs Wilson, the Jamaica goalie, covered her eyes. Mr Wilson had his back to Jamie's dad. He pulled the ball backwards between his legs, turned – and fell over the ball. Jamie's dad hit a pass to little Max, who controlled it neatly and shot past Mrs Wilson.

'One nil to Iceland and half time,' Marshall said. 'Nice move, Roy,' he said to Mr Wilson. 'Shame it didn't come off!'

Matt was doing a little celebration dance. He stopped quickly when Lou punched him. Luckily the ref didn't see.

In the second half, Jamaica attacked all

the time. It was easy to attack, because Matt didn't dare to tackle Lou, but it was impossible to score, because Jamie stopped every one of Jamaica's shots.

'He is just brilliant!' said Tulsi to Rafi. 'He didn't have to move and he stopped everything. Even TJ's hardest shots. Just think – if he wasn't full of food . . .'

'Hey!' said Rafi. 'Why did we never think of that before? It's exactly what we need. A goalie who stops everything!'

'But he'll never do it,' Tulsi said. 'Why would he want to?'

'Maybe because everyone thinks he's fantastic,' said Rafi, as Iceland celebrated victory over Jamaica. Jamie's team had a lot of supporters and they were all congratulating him.

'I tried,' said TJ to his sister, as they walked off the pitch. 'I really did.'

Iceland went on to defeat India in the final. The match was 0–0 after extra time, and Iceland won 2–0 on penalties. Not even Tulsi could score past Jamie. There was no doubt at all who was the man of the match.

When Jamie went up to receive the trophy, Marshall shook him by the hand.

'A star is born!' he said.

# Parkview World Cup

Match ① ②③ 12.30   Match ④⑤⑥ 12.40   Match ⑦⑧ 12.50

Quarter Finals ①② 1.00   ③④ 1.15

Semi Finals ① 1.30   ② 1.45

Final   2.00

| First Round | Quarter Finals | Semi Final |

① Portugal 1
  USA 0

Portugal 1
①

Portugal 0

② Spain 2
  England 0

Spain 0

India 0

③ India 4
  Mexico 0

India 3
②

India 2

④ China 7
  Nigeria 3

China 1

Iceland win
2-0 on penalties

⑤ Argentina 1
  France 2

France 1
③

⑥ Scotland 1
  Iceland 3

Iceland 2

Iceland 1

⑦ Jamaica 6
  Brazil 0

Jamaica 3
④

Iceland 0

⑧ Australia 3
  Ivory coast 2

Australia 0

Jamaica 0

# CHAPTER 10

'Dad reckons if he gets fit enough from his runs, he might join a football team himself,' TJ said one night, the week after the World Cup. Jamie, Rob and TJ were waiting at TJ's house while his dad changed into his running kit.

'I don't think that move of his would work even if he was fit,' said Rob.

TJ laughed. 'Probably not,' he said. 'But he did do it once – we've got video evidence – so maybe he'll do it again one day.'

'How's the diet going, Jamie?' asked TJ's mum.

'Good,' said Jamie. 'Mum's got loads of new recipes from the World Cup day. We've had something different every night this week.'

'But not too much, I hope. Didn't you overdo it a bit before the World Cup?'

'I won't do that again,' Jamie said with a grin. 'And anyway, we've been having lots of salads. I don't think you can actually get fat from eating too much salad, can you?'

'I doubt it,' Mrs Wilson said with a smile.

Jamie laughed. 'Well, I'm not going to,' he said, with a determined look on his face.

'And how about you, Rob?' Mrs Wilson asked. 'Does all this running mean you're going to give up collecting the statistics?'

'I'm doing that too,' Rob said earnestly, holding up a small plastic object. 'This is a pedometer. It counts how far we run.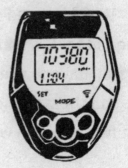

And I've got my stopwatch too.'

'We'd better get started then,' laughed Mr Wilson, coming into the room in a brand-new tracksuit and trainers. 'No time to waste.'

They parked at the Sports Centre and jogged off along the trail.

'You're not out of breath,' TJ said to Jamie, when they'd run nearly a kilometre.

'No,' agreed Jamie. 'Do you think Mr Wood will put me back in the team now?' There was an uncomfortable silence, as they jogged on. 'Well?' said Jamie. 'I did all right at training last night, didn't I?'

'So did everyone else,' Rob said finally.

'And Mr Wood's already selected the squad for the match against Wasps. I expect you'll have to wait. Probably being a goalie is your best chance.'

'What, like TJ was? It's a rubbish job, isn't

it, TJ? You couldn't wait to stop doing it.'

'It wasn't that bad,' said TJ.

'But you were good in the World Cup, Jamie,' Rob insisted.

'That was just for fun. And to stop my stomach from exploding.'

'I'm only saying,' said Rob, as they arrived back at the car park. He looked at his pedometer. 'That was three point one kilometres,' he said. 'It took twenty-one minutes. It's a big improvement. We should probably have a complete training schedule planned out. I'll do it if you like.'

'There's no point in all this,' muttered Jamie. 'Not if I can't get in the team.'

'You are going to come to the match on Sunday though, aren't you?' TJ said. 'To support us? Rob's coming and he isn't playing either.'

'I don't know,' Jamie said. 'I haven't decided yet.'

On Sunday morning a large white minibus
was waiting for them at the school. Mr Wood
and Miss Berry were standing outside the
gate, and TJ was surprised to see Mr Burrows
waiting there with them. 'I thought I'd come
along and give you a little support,' he said.
'When I watched you beat Hillside, well, it
was jolly exciting. I rather enjoyed it.'

The Wasps ground was in a small town
about six miles out into the countryside.
They drove through a housing estate and
parked in a narrow road that was full of cars.
Small boys and girls were getting out of the
cars in their football boots and making their
way through a wooden gate.

'It's huge!' exclaimed Rafi, as they made
their way through the gate onto the playing
field. There were three small pitches marked
out nearby, and beyond a line of trees they
saw more pitches, where games had already

begun. Mr Wood led the way to a low brick clubhouse and into their dressing room.

'Find a peg and hang your things up,' he said. 'Girls, there's a room for you next door. Miss Berry will show you. Then we'll go and find our pitch.'

Only Tulsi wasn't nervous. 'I play here every year,' she said. 'It's the biggest youth soccer club in the area. They have lots and lots of teams, and most of them are good.'

'Why has Mr Wood brought us here?' said Leila. 'I mean, why couldn't we start by playing a team that wasn't very good?'

'Don't worry,' said Rob. 'Mr Wood knows what he's doing.'

'OK,' said Mr Wood. 'We're on the end pitch. I'll show you. And don't look so worried. It'll be fun.'

They walked past two other games where very small kids were playing. 'They look like Jamie's brother,' TJ said, and then wished he hadn't, because it made them all think about Jamie. TJ really missed him. It didn't seem the same without him.

They reached their pitch and the Wasps team were warming up at the far end in their orange and black striped shirts. The Parkview shirts were blue and black, and very old. Cameron's dad had mended them for their match against Hillside, but some of the mending was coming undone. Also, there were only six shirts and one goalie top.

'It's a shame that the new kit hasn't arrived yet,' Mr Wood said. 'If I bring on a sub, you'll just have to change over. Now, let's get warmed up.'

As they went through their routines, TJ couldn't help glancing at the Wasps team. They were all boys. Mr Wood had explained that Sunday League teams weren't usually mixed.

'It won't matter,' he said, looking at Tulsi

and Leila. 'Just remember who was the fittest person on the beep test.'

But even so, the Wasps team looked big and strong. They were hitting the ball to each other very hard, and controlling it effortlessly.

'Just remember what I've taught you,' Mr Wood said. 'Rafi, I'd like you to be captain for this game. You can beat them, Parkview! I'm sure of it.'

# CHAPTER 11

'It's not right without Jamie,' TJ said to Tulsi, as he stood over the ball waiting to kick off. Rafi had won the toss.

'I know,' Tulsi said. 'It feels as if we haven't got enough players.' She glanced back at the rest of their team. Rafi and Rodrigo were in midfield, and Tommy and Leila in defence, with Danny waiting in goal. Their subs, Ariyan and Cameron, were at the side, warming up in case they had to come on. 'Remember how Jamie tackled Krissy Barton in our first match?'

TJ smiled. Krissy was the best striker

# Parkview Team Sheet

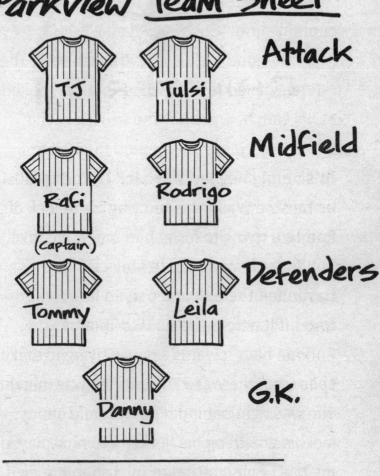

**Attack**

TJ      Tulsi

**Midfield**

Rafi      Rodrigo
(captain)

**Defenders**

Tommy      Leila

**G.K.**

Danny

---

Ariyan    Cameron     **Subs**

Hillside had, but Jamie had been too strong for her.

'Come on, Parkside,' called Rafi, doing his captain's job. 'Good luck, Leila.'

'Yeah, good luck, Leila,' they all said. The referee waved to his two assistants, looked at his watch, and blew the whistle. Leila smiled nervously. TJ touched the ball to Tulsi, and she played it back to Rodrigo. Instantly a Wasp was buzzing around Rodrigo, trying to hurry him into a mistake, but Rodrigo managed to stay calm. He controlled the ball and played it to Rafi, who hit it across the field to Tommy.

TJ ran back towards Tommy, trying to make space, but the Wasps player who was marking him was right behind him. He could almost feel his breath on his neck. As Tommy played the ball to him, he heard Tulsi shouting for it, and out of the corner of his eye he saw her making a darting run forward. Tommy had hit the ball hard and true.

TJ acted instinctively. Instead of controlling it and looking for a pass, he let it flick off the outside of his heel, so that it flew past one side of the defender towards Tulsi, as he spun to run the other side.

If it had worked, it would have been brilliant.

But it failed.

As TJ ran down the wing, hoping that Tulsi would play the ball back into his path, he saw the tall, black-haired defender who was marking her step forward and intercept his pass. And now both TJ and Tulsi were out of position. TJ heard his marker laugh, as he raced away from him to join in the Wasps attack. He knew that it was his job to follow him back, but the Wasps player had ten metres start on him and even TJ wasn't that fast. The ball was out on the Wasps left wing now, and there was nothing Leila could do to stop the Wasps winger from crossing it. The player TJ should have been marking stepped forward and smashed the ball into the net.

'What did you do that for?' demanded Danny, as he handed TJ the ball. 'You just gave it away. And you should have got back.'

'I know. I'm sorry. Don't worry, Leila. There was nothing you could do.'

'Hey, TJ,' said Rafi. 'It was OK. It was a great idea.'

But TJ shook his head. He knew it had been a bad decision. Mr Wood had told them they would have to be patient and defend well, and he'd gone and done something really stupid.

'Come on, lad,' called a voice from the touchline. 'Get your head up. There's a long way to go yet.'

TJ turned and saw Mr Coggins, the caretaker, standing with Mr Burrows.

Janice the dinner lady was there too, and quite a few mums and dads had made the journey. He hadn't expected them all to be here. They must have arrived while the team were warming up.

'You can do it, Parkview,' yelled Janice.

This time Tulsi passed the ball back to Rafi. When Rafi saw the Wasps captain bearing down on him, he forgot all his training and started to run with the ball. He took it past Rodrigo, then saw another Wasps player coming towards him, and did a fancy turn before dribbling off in the opposite direction. There were Wasps players all around him now.

'Clear it, Rafi,' yelled Tommy, but Rafi had run out of space. A Wasps player blocked the ball with his foot and Rafi went tumbling over.

With three crisp passes the Wasps had the ball on the edge of the penalty area, and there was nothing Danny could do to stop them scoring. It was 2–0 to Wasps and they had only been playing for two minutes.

'You're all rubbish,' Danny said angrily, as he chucked the ball to Tommy. 'If I didn't have to be in goal I'd show you how to tackle.'

'All you had to do was pass it,' Tulsi said to Rafi.

'Yeah, I know,' Rafi said. 'I just panicked. I couldn't help it.'

'There's no point arguing,' said TJ. 'We just have to play better, that's all.'

'Go on, then,' Tulsi replied, tapping the ball to him. 'You show us.'

TJ passed to Rodrigo, who played it neatly out wide to Leila. 'That's better, Parkview!' called Mr Wood. 'Keep passing it! Don't let them rush you.'

Leila hit a neat pass to TJ and he looked around quickly, trying to find someone to give the ball to. It was no good. The only clear space he could see was back to Danny in goal.

'Here, Danny,' he yelled, and hit the pass towards him.

Too late, TJ saw the Wasps captain. He had anticipated TJ's pass and he was racing after the ball.

Danny saw the danger, but TJ knew that there was no way he could reach the ball before the Wasps player did. It was like watching a car crash. Danny was desperate. He leaped towards the Wasps captain, feet first, and the Wasps player crashed to the ground like a fallen tree.

There was a moment's silence, followed by yells of anger from the Wasps supporters.

The Wasps captain was lying on the ground, groaning, and the Wasps trainer ran onto the pitch.

'I hardly touched him,' Danny said.

'I don't very often have to do this,' the ref

said. 'Not with kids your age. You never had any intention of going for the ball, young man. Everyone here could see that. So I've no choice but to send you off.' He pulled the red card from his pocket, and showed it to Danny.

'Do what you like,' muttered Danny, as he walked off the pitch.

'I'm sorry, Danny,' TJ said, as he walked past him. 'It was a bad pass.'

Danny didn't even look at him. 'I don't care about this stupid team anyway,' he said. 'I hope you lose.'

# CHAPTER 12

Mr Wood watched Danny walk towards the dressing room, then he said something to Miss Berry and she went after Danny. Mr Wood turned back to the Wasps coach. 'I'm sorry about that, Brian,' he said. 'I don't know what got into the lad.'

The coach was kneeling beside the Wasps captain, spraying something on his leg. 'Give us a few moments, will you?' he said.

Mr Wood called the Parkview squad together. 'We need a new goalkeeper,' he said. 'Who's it going to be?'

They all looked at each other. None of them wanted to go in goal. 'How about you, TJ? You're the only one who's done it before.'

TJ knew it was the only sensible solution, but he still felt sick. Everything was going wrong. He was just reaching out to take the gloves from Mr Wood when Tulsi said, 'Look. There's Jamie.'

Jamie was standing on the far side of the pitch with his dad and his little brothers, Max and Cody.

'Jamie could go in goal,' Rafi said. 'He's really good.'

'He was good in the World Cup, you mean,' said Tommy. 'That doesn't mean he'd be good in a proper match.'

'Jamie isn't even in the squad,' Mr Wood said. 'And he's not fit. And he probably hasn't got any kit.'

'Actually,' said Rob, 'Jamie ran three point

one kilometres in just over twenty minutes last week. So he's much fitter than he was a few weeks ago. And he's wearing a tracksuit and trainers.'

'Are you serious, Rob?' Mr Wood said. 'I know Jamie's looking fitter, but you really think he could play in goal?'

Rob nodded.

'And you all agree?'

They all did.

'Well, you go and ask him if he'll do it, Rob,' Mr Wood said. 'And, Cameron, go and get the goalkeeper's shirt from Danny. Be quick. I'll ask the Wasps coach if he minds an unorthodox substitution. After what just happened he might not like the idea.'

Rob returned with Jamie. 'Well?' Mr Wood asked him. 'Will you do it, Jamie? The Wasps don't mind.'

'I don't . . . I mean, this doesn't mean I have to be a goalie for ever and ever, does it?' Jamie asked.

Mr Wood shook his head. 'Just do your best,' he said.

Jamie grinned. 'OK, then,' he said. 'I'll have a go.'

'Right,' said Mr Wood, as the Wasps captain struggled to his feet out on the pitch. 'You realize I'm going to have to take one of you off?'

None of them had thought of that. Jamie could only come on as a substitute. 'I think it'll have to be you, Rodrigo,' Mr Wood said. 'We can't take a defender off, and if we're going to get back in the game we're going to need our strikers. Rafi, you'll be in midfield on your own, but Tulsi and TJ will come back and help you. You're all going to have a lot of running to do.'

'Good luck, Jamie,' Rodrigo said, as he walked over to the touchline and Cameron ran up with the goalie's top. Jamie pulled the top over his head.

'Look at that,' said TJ. 'It fits! You must have got thinner, Jamie.'

'I'm sorry, Rodrigo,' Jamie said. 'I didn't know he'd take you off.'

'OK, everyone,' Mr Wood said. 'This is going to be very hard work, but I don't want you to just defend. If you do that, they'll keep on scoring goals. You have to attack them. Take them by surprise. But first you've got a free kick to defend.'

They made their way back onto the pitch.

'OK, Leroy?' the Wasps coach said to his captain.

Leroy walked a few steps and then nodded. 'I'll be fine,' he said. TJ could see the angry red marks on his thigh where Danny's boots had scraped.

Jamie stood between the goalposts and clapped his hands. 'Come on, Parkview,' he yelled. 'We can beat this lot.'

TJ saw the Wasps players around him laughing, but just looking at Jamie standing there in goal made him feel better. Rafi, Tommy and Leila made a wall on the edge of the penalty area. The ref blew his whistle and Leroy took the free kick. It bent around the wall and into the top corner of the net.

Even Jamie couldn't do anything except watch it. It was a perfect free kick.

'Don't worry, Parkview,' Jamie yelled, as he threw the ball back to the centre circle. 'We beat Hillside, didn't we? We were three nil down then, and we won it.'

There was a ripple of applause from the small group of Parkview supporters on the touchline. 'Come on, Parkview,' Mr Burrows yelled. 'You can do it!'

'We have to move more,' TJ said to Tulsi.

'We have to confuse them a bit. We can swap places sometimes, and we have to help Rafi make tackles.'

Tulsi nodded her agreement.

They kicked off. Rafi raced into space and received a pass. He took the lightest of touches and then laid the ball off to TJ. TJ didn't even need to take a touch. He saw Tommy moving forward and tapped the ball to him. Tommy moved it on smoothly to Tulsi, who was close to the Wasps penalty area with her back to the goal. She controlled the ball and shielded it from the defender behind her, as Rafi and TJ ran towards the penalty area, then she played a pass into TJ's path. TJ flicked the ball past the defender, catching him by surprise, and sprinted for the goal line. He heard his brother, Joey, yell, 'Go on, TJ!' and he knew the Wasps defender would never catch him.

He hit his cross hard across the penalty

area – but there was no one there.

The ball flashed harmlessly between the Wasps defenders and their goalie and went out for a throw-in on the other side of the pitch.

'Where were you?' he said to Tulsi.

'You didn't look, did you?' she said.

'No, but it was a perfect cross. You should have known what I'd do.'

'Oh, what, I'm supposed to be a mind-reader now, am I?'

'Stop it, you two,' yelled Rafi. 'Get back!'

Wasps had taken the throw-in quickly and the black-haired defender was running forward with the ball at his feet. TJ sprinted after him, breathing hard. Rafi didn't know whether to mark Leroy, or go and challenge the running defender. There seemed to be Wasps players everywhere. Just as TJ caught up with the defender he struck his shot, and TJ saw the ball rocketing towards the top left-hand corner. It was a certain goal.

But then Jamie took off. No one else in the team could have reached the ball, but Jamie stretched out his fingertips and pushed it over the bar. Everyone on the pitch stared, as Jamie rolled on the ground and then stood up with a streak of mud on his face.

'Brilliant save, lad,' said the ref, as he pointed to the corner flag.

'JAMIE, JAMIE!' chanted the Parkview fans.

'Don't just stand there,' Jamie yelled. 'Defend!'

They all ran back into the penalty area, as Leroy took the corner, but Jamie didn't need them. 'Keeper's!' he yelled, and he jumped through the swarm of Wasps players to pull the ball out of the air, as the ref blew the whistle for half time.

# CHAPTER 13

'I'm amazed,' said Mr Wood to Jamie, as he handed out slices of orange. 'That's one of the best saves I've ever seen.' TJ was almost sure that Jamie blushed.

'We're still losing three nil though,' Rafi pointed out.

'Yes, but you are starting to play some good football,' Mr Wood replied. 'And I've got a feeling that your fitness training might be paying off. You were making them work quite hard and one or two of them were starting to puff a little.'

'They think they've already won,' Rob said, as he handed out the water bottles. 'Look at them.'

The Wasps players were standing around laughing with their mums and dads. Some of them were drinking Coke and TJ saw one of them with an ice cream. Then the Wasps coach, Brian, came out of the dressing room with Leroy, who now had a big white bandage around his thigh. When Brian saw what was happening, his face darkened and they heard him shouting at the players, waving their mums and dads away.

'You're right, Rob,' Mr Wood said with a grin. 'A lot of teams get over-confident when they're three nil up, and it looks like they're as human as anyone else.'

'They've still got an extra player,' TJ pointed out.

'I think the Coke and ice cream should just about cancel that out,' Mr Wood told them. 'Let's really give them something to think about.'

Wasps kicked off, and straight away they were on the attack, zipping the ball from player to player before the Parkview players could get near it. They passed it out to the right wing, where a skinny black boy dribbled forward to take on Tommy. 'Pass it, Martin,' yelled the Wasps coach, but Martin paid no attention. In the first half he had never once tried to beat Tommy with the ball, but now he was over-confident and he started to show off. He stepped over it once, then twice, then dragged it back with the sole of his foot and flicked it with the outside of his right boot.

Tommy didn't watch Martin's fancy foot-work. He just watched the ball, and when Martin tried to go past him he simply reached out a foot and took the ball away from him. There were groans from the Wasps supporters, as Tommy clipped the ball to Rafi, who had been darting backwards and forwards trying to lose his marker and had managed to find a few metres of space. Rafi dragged the ball backwards away from the Wasps player who was trying to tackle him.

Tulsi was running diagonally away from him with her marker trailing behind her.

Rafi had to judge the pass carefully. If he hit it too hard it would run out of play before Tulsi could catch it, and if it wasn't hard enough then the defender would get it. He struck the ball just the way Mr Wood had shown him in training, chipping it so that it would be spinning backwards as it hit the ground, and would slow up just a little.

Tulsi saw the ball dropping over her head and she sprinted after it. 'Our throw!' yelled the Wasps fans, as she controlled the ball right on the line and moved off down the wing, but the linesman's flag stayed down.

Tulsi had kept the ball in play, and now she looked up and saw TJ running towards the penalty area. She curved her pass into his path so that he didn't have to pause in his run, but there was still the tall, black-haired defender in his way.

TJ took one touch, and he saw the hesitation in the defender's eyes. Then the defender burped, very loudly, and in a split

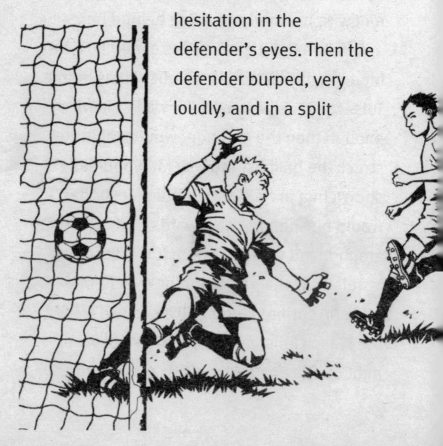

second TJ had skipped past him and buried the ball in the net, low to the goalkeeper's left.

The Parkview fans screamed and shouted as if they had won the match. 'Concentrate, Parkview,' yelled Mr Wood, as TJ grabbed the ball from the net and ran back to place it on the centre spot. 'That was good work. Don't waste it!'

TJ looked over as Mr Wood spoke and saw a stocky man in a grey puffa jacket and a red woolly hat standing beside him, saying something. Mr Wood nodded in agreement. TJ knew that he'd seen the man somewhere very recently, but he couldn't remember where. 'Who's that?' he asked Tulsi, as they waited for

Wasps to restart the game.

Tulsi shrugged. 'Some friend of Mr Wood's, I expect. Come on, let's get another one.'

'Keep going, Wasps,' called one of their supporters. 'Show 'em how you can sting!'

Leroy didn't need any encouragement. TJ could see that he was angry they'd conceded a goal. Straight from the kick-off, he took the ball and headed down the middle of the pitch towards Jamie's goal. He took Rafi completely by surprise, and brushed off his weak tackle as if he hadn't even noticed him. He was clean through on goal.

But Jamie was there. He had seen what was happening and moved quickly off his line. Now, as Leroy pulled back his foot to shoot, Jamie threw himself, full-length, on the ground at Leroy's feet. The shot cannoned into his stomach at point-blank range, but Jamie jumped quickly to his feet and rolled the ball to Tommy.

Tommy saw his chance and raced past two stunned Wasps players before they had time to move. Then, as they ran towards him, he played the ball across the width of the pitch to Leila, who hit a first-time pass to TJ. TJ could see the fear in the eyes of the black-haired defender. Another defender was coming to help him, but that left Tulsi completely unmarked. TJ simply passed the ball between the two defenders, and Tulsi lashed her shot past the goalkeeper.

TJ ran all the way back to Jamie and whacked him on the back. 'Brilliant, Jamie,' he said. 'We'd probably be losing five nil if it wasn't for you. And that was a great pass, Leila.'

Leila went bright red. Jamie's brothers were jumping around on the touchline, chanting his name. As TJ ran past them, he saw a Wasps supporter pointing at the other side of the pitch, where Mr Wood was standing with the man in the red hat.

'He's a scout from Wanderers,' the man said. 'I've seen him down here before.'

TJ felt his heart pounding. He saw the buzz spreading along the touchline, as the spectators realized there was a scout watching. If Parkview kept playing well then any of them might have a chance to get into the Wanderers Academy. TJ hardly dared to think it, but it might even be him.

# CHAPTER 14

It was 3–2 to Wasps, as they kicked off again, and the noise of the crowd was loud in TJ's ears. The game must be nearly over, but he hadn't seen the referee look at his watch yet. And he suddenly felt nervous. What if he played badly? What if he made a mistake?

'TJ,' yelled Rafi. 'Wake up!'

TJ realized he'd let Rafi's pass slide past him into touch. He shook himself and held up a hand to say sorry. He raced after the Wasps player who had the ball and tackled him, winning it back. As he moved away, he could hear that the player he'd tackled was breathing hard. He played it back to Rafi, who passed it on to Tommy. TJ could see that all the Wasps players were struggling. Maybe it was the food and drink they'd had at half time, or maybe Mr Wood's fitness training was paying off. We're going to get a draw, he thought – and then he saw the ref look at his watch.

Suddenly he knew that he could beat the flagging Wasps defenders. He ran into the centre circle, calling for the ball, and Tommy passed it. A defender had followed him, but TJ touched the ball into space with the outside of his boot and left the defender stranded as he tore after it. He felt exhilarated, as if he could run all day. He saw another defender approaching, swayed one way, and moved the opposite way, all at top speed.

And now he could see the goal, and the

keeper coming out towards him. He picked his spot, right inside the far post. His world seemed to focus down to that tiny point where he wanted the ball to go, and he struck it as hard as he knew how.

He knew it was right from the moment it left his boot. There was nothing the goalkeeper could do to stop it – and it was the last kick of the match. They had drawn with Wasps!

It was only when the celebrations had died down that TJ remembered the scout. He looked around for him, but he'd gone. TJ shrugged to himself. He'd been stupid, anyway, to get worked up about that. It had been a great game, and it looked as if they had found a brilliant goalkeeper. Although Jamie didn't seem so sure.

'I like tackling people,' he said, when the tenth person had told him what a terrific keeper he was. 'I like shooting.'

'Yeah, but you're better at being a goalie,' said Rob. 'You're a good tackler, but you're an excellent keeper.'

'Maybe,' said Jamie. 'But it would have been better if Danny hadn't lost his temper. I'd rather be a defender.'

'Where is Danny anyway?' asked TJ. He felt guilty about his back pass. That was what had started the trouble after all. 'I'll be back,' he said, and he ran over to the dressing room.

Danny was changed and sitting in the corner with his eyes closed. He didn't look angry any more, just a bit sad. 'Hey, Danny,' TJ said. 'I'm sorry about the back pass. It was tough luck getting sent off like that.'

Danny looked up. 'I suppose you're all pleased now,' he said. 'None of you wanted me in the team in the first place.'

'That's not true . . .'

'Of course it is. You're new, so you don't

116

know anything. Why don't you go away and leave me alone.'

TJ turned to go out of the door. He paused. 'We drew,' he said. 'Three all.'

But Danny didn't reply.

Out on the field an excited knot of players and parents were walking towards the dressing rooms. Mr Burrows' face was flushed. 'A magnificent fight back,' he was saying. 'It really gives me hope. If you can take on the mighty Meadow Green Wasps, then I really think there's no reason we can't see off those terrible inspectors.'

Mr Burrows' excitement was infectious, but TJ still didn't feel right. While they were changing he couldn't help noticing Danny sitting alone in the corner. No one said a word to him. And TJ realized that Jamie didn't look too happy either.

'What's up?' asked his dad when TJ came out of the dressing room and walked over to his family. 'You should be over the moon. You just scored two brilliant goals.'

'I know,' said TJ. 'But not everyone's happy. Look at Jamie. Look at Danny.'

'Well,' said TJ's dad, 'Jamie looks like a natural-born keeper to me, so I guess he'll just have to get used to it. And as for Danny, it was a nasty challenge. The ref didn't have any choice, you know.'

'It's not that,' TJ replied. 'It's just, I know Danny can be a bit of a bully, but no one seems to like him, and I feel sorry for him.'

Mr Wilson looked at TJ, then he ruffled his hair in a way that made TJ feel embarrassed and pleased at the same time. 'If you feel like that, son, then I think you'll find a way to work things out,' his dad said. 'We can talk about it later if you like. But right now I reckon we should celebrate. You were out for the count and you came back against the mighty Wasps. It was fantastic!'

# CHAPTER 15

On Monday morning when they filed into
assembly, TJ saw that Mrs Hubbard, the
school cook, was sitting on a chair beside
Mr Burrows.

'From today,' Mr Burrows announced, 'we
are going to have new, healthy school
meals. Mrs Hubbard is going to tell you all
about it.'

Mrs Hubbard stood up. Everyone clapped
and cheered and her face went very red. 'It's
all because of that World Food Day,' she
said, once Mr Burrows had made them all be
quiet. 'I collected lots of recipes, and me

and my ladies in the kitchen have been trying them out. So today all of you can try them out too.'

There was loud clapping and quite a lot of yelling from the little ones. When they filed out of the hall TJ could already smell the lunch being cooked. Jamie groaned. 'How will I keep fit if we have even more delicious lunches?' he said.

'They're going to be healthy,' Tulsi told him. 'Weren't you listening?'

And when they went into the dining hall at lunch time, there were lots of salads and delicious-looking vegetables and curry, and no chips or burgers at all.

'Brilliant, Mrs Hubbard,' Rafi said. 'Can I have that tropical fruit for afters, please?'

'Of course,' Mrs Hubbard said proudly. 'And where's my friend, Jamie? Oh, there you are, love. Look what I've got for you.'

She reached under the shiny metal

counter and pulled out a steaming pot of shepherd's pie. 'Just a little something extra,' she said. 'You look like you need building up so I reckon you need a bit more than these others.'

'Mrs Hubbard, you can't!' exclaimed Tulsi. 'You'll spoil everything!'

Mrs Hubbard's face fell. 'It's all very well, all this healthy food,' she said. 'I do like it, but people like me and my husband, and young Jamie, we need a little more. We're big-boned, you see.'

'Thanks, Mrs Hubbard,' said Jamie, and for an awful moment TJ thought he was going to take the pie. 'But I really want to be in the team. I have to eat the right food. Can I just have the spicy chicken and rice, please? And some of that salad.'

'Hey, well done, Jamie,' Tulsi said, high-fiving him.

'I want to get my old place back,' Jamie replied, as they made their way to a table.

'I'm going to be so fit that Mr Wood will *have* to make me a defender again.'

That night, at training, Jamie worked harder than anyone. When they ran round the field to warm up, he kept up with Mr Wood easily. Then when they did sprints Jamie powered his way backwards and forwards until the sweat was rolling down his face and soaking his shirt. They went on to do some simple pass and control exercises, and TJ worked with Jamie as usual.

'Do you think Mr Wood has noticed?' asked Jamie. 'He can't say I'm not fit now.'

'No,' agreed TJ, as they moved the ball backwards and forwards in one of the ten-metre squares that had been marked out on the field. 'But you'll have to pass better than that,' he added, laughing, as he raced after yet another one of Jamie's random passes.

'I'm a destroyer,' Jamie grinned. 'Some

# TJ, Rob, Jamie, Mr Wilson & Joey's
## Run times and distances

① 1.3 Km    12m 15 sec

② 1.5 Km    13m 32 sec    Week 1

③ 1.5 km    12 m 20 sec

---

④ 1.8 Km    14m

⑤ 1.8 Km    13m 40 sec    Week 2

⑥ 2 Km    15m 13 sec

---

⑦ 2.5Km    19m 01 sec

⑧ 2.5Km    18m 20 sec    Week 3

⑨ 3 Km    23m 07 sec

---

⑩ 3.1 Km    21m    Week 4

one else can take care of the fancy passes. I tackle them and belt it clear.'

TJ glanced around the field. Everyone was working just as hard as they were. He saw Rob working with Leila. Rob had kept up with them easily on their runs, and now he was passing and controlling the ball very well. Better than a lot of the others, in fact.

'Right,' said Mr Wood, 'I'd like one of you to throw the ball to your partner, and the other one to play the ball back first time. You can use your head, or your feet, or your chest. Just try to get the ball accurately back to your partner first time, OK?'

'Why don't I throw to you?' Jamie said to TJ. 'You'll be good at this.'

Jamie was right about that. TJ had no problem getting the ball back to Jamie and it didn't matter how high or fast Jamie threw it.

'Nice work, TJ,' Mr Wood said, as he passed by. 'Swap over now, boys, and let's see what Jamie can do.'

TJ took the ball and threw it to Jamie.
He tried to make sure it reached Jamie at
a perfect height. He aimed to make it easy,
but when Jamie swung his foot at the ball
it flew off and hit Tulsi on the back of the
head, two squares away.

'Hey!' she yelled, then she turned and
saw Jamie and laughed. 'I might have
guessed,' she said.

'I'll never get it right,' muttered Jamie.

'You should practise like I do,' TJ said.
'I bang it against the wall and try to hit it
back. I try to surprise myself.'

'But I do practise,' Jamie said. 'It doesn't
matter what I do, I can't get better. I've broken
four windows and three flowerpots too. I
won't have any pocket money for years.'

'Just keep your eye on the ball,' TJ said,
chucking it to him again. 'See? That's better.'

'You're right,' Jamie said, brightening.

'Throw me another one.'

TJ threw, and Jamie swung his leg. The ball flew way up into the air and came down in the street on the other side of the fence.

'You know what?' TJ told him. 'You really are a dodgy defender. You have to admit it. But you're a great goalie.'

'TJ's right,' said Mr Wood, who had been watching. 'You can tackle, Jamie, and you've got yourself very fit. But I think goalie is your best position, and I think you're easily the best goalie we have. So how about it? Will you be our goalkeeper?'

They all waited. 'Go on, Jamie,' pleaded Tulsi. 'You really are a brilliant keeper.'

'And we need you,' said Rafi.

'Please,' said Rodrigo.

Jamie shook his head and grinned. 'OK, then,' he said. 'But I'm going to keep practising my passing. I still think I'll be a defender one day.'

# CHAPTER 16

On the morning of the District Tournament a
big convoy of cars assembled at the school,
ready to follow the Parkview team in their
minibus to the nearby town, where the
tournament was taking place.

'Look,' said Rafi to TJ, as they were waiting
to get on the minibus, 'Mrs Hubbard and the
cooks have joined up with Janice and the
dinner ladies.'

'And they've got new pom-poms too!' said
Tulsi. 'In our colours!'

'It's not just us who've got new stuff,'
Janice said. 'Look, here comes Mr B.'

Mr Burrows was carrying two enormous sports bags. He unzipped one and pulled out a football shirt. 'We have shirts, shorts, socks, shin pads and even some of these.' He opened the second holdall and took out a bundle of waterproof jackets. He held one up. On the back it said:

## ORCHARDS GARDEN CENTRE.

'You can thank our new Parents and Friends Association for organizing these,' Mr Burrows said. 'It was their idea to look for a sponsor for the team. And the Garden Centre helped us fix our pitch so they were very keen.'

'Awesome,' said Tulsi. 'This is even better than my Sunday League team's kit.'

'It's great,' said Mr Wood, 'but a nice kit isn't going to win football matches. Are you all here now? I hope you've got the right shoes. You've remembered we're playing on Astroturf?'

He called out their names. It was seven-a-side again, so there were ten of them in the squad: Jamie in goal, Tommy, Ariyan and Leila as defenders, Rafi, Rodrigo – who was their captain for today – and Cameron in midfield, and TJ, Tulsi and Jay up front. As they climbed into the minibus, the cheerleaders were singing 'We Are the Champions.'

'I don't like it,' TJ said to Jamie, who was sitting next to him. 'They all seem to think we've already won. We've only played two proper matches ever. We're just as likely to lose every game.'

The car park at the tournament was full of coaches and cars and teams and supporters. TJ could see that everyone in the Parkview squad was feeling nervous. Then he saw Leroy, the Wasps captain. 'What's he doing here?' he asked.

'He plays for Meadow Green School,' Rob said. 'Almost all the Wasps team go to Meadow Green School. They won their schools league last season, just like Hillside won ours.'

'There's Hillside over there,' Rafi said. 'They'll be looking for revenge. They really hated it when we beat them.'

Out on the pitches, corner flags fluttered in the chilly breeze. 'There's Marshall,' said Rob, pointing. 'He's come to support us.'

Sure enough, Marshall was walking towards them, with his beanie pulled low over his eyes and an outsize hoodie pulled over the top of that.

'He's in disguise again,' laughed Tommy. 'I don't know why he bothers. Someone's bound to recognize him.'

But, for the moment, no one had. 'It's Saturday,' TJ said to Marshall. 'Haven't you got a game today?'

'Not this week,' Marshall replied, after saying hello to everyone.

'But you played for Wanderers last week,' said TJ. 'So why . . . ?'

'I'm not fully fit yet,' Marshall said. 'I was subbed at half time last week. It takes a long time to get back to full fitness after an injury like mine. But it's a great chance for me to watch some football today. I love the kit. You look terrific.'

'We don't feel that great,' Tulsi said, speaking for all of them. 'All these people have come to watch us, and they all think we're going to win easily.'

'Hey, how do you think I feel every week?' Marshall said. 'Everyone gets nervous. You just have to think how lucky you are to be playing football at all.'

Parkview were playing on Pitch Seven, right at the far end. The Parkview supporters made a big camp by the fence, as Mr Wood,

Marshall and Miss Berry took the squad away to warm up.

'We play three matches in this part of the tournament,' Mr Wood told them, when they were ready. 'And between the first two games we only have a ten-minute break, so I'll be using the whole squad. Ariyan, Jay, Cameron – you're the subs for the first match. The team we're playing are called Swinburne School. I don't know anything about them, but we don't need to worry about who we play. We're as good as anyone here. Even the mighty Wasps couldn't beat us. Off you go. The ref's waiting.'

They ran onto the pitch and Rodrigo won the toss. The Parkview fans were making a huge amount of noise on the touchline, as Tulsi stroked the ball to TJ and he played it back to Rafi. Straight away, a Swinburne player tackled Rafi and the ball squirted into touch. Swinburne attacked from the throw-in, but Tommy chased after the striker and poked the ball across to Rodrigo as he was about to shoot.

Rodrigo passed to Rafi again, but once more Rafi was tackled. 'More quick, Rafi!' Rodrigo said, but it wasn't that easy. The Swinburne team were all excellent tacklers, and the Parkview defenders found it almost impossible to get the ball to TJ and Tulsi. The game was no fun to play in, and TJ could see from the faces of the spectators that it was no fun to watch either. 'They're very good at defending,' Mr Wood said at half time.

'But they haven't managed a single shot,' Rob said. 'Maybe we should push Rafi forward a bit.'

'Just what I was thinking,' Mr Wood replied. 'And I'm going to bring Ariyan on for Tommy and Cameron for Leila. You've done well, you two, but you've had to do a lot of running.'

The second half continued just like the first. The Swinburne strikers managed a couple of shots, but Jamie saved them easily. 'Go on, Rafi,' he said, as he rolled the ball out to Rodrigo. 'Get forward!'

Rodrigo looked up and saw TJ moving down the wing. For the first time in the game, Rodrigo's marker had given him some space – enough space for him to push the ball forward a few metres and then hit a high pass across the field to TJ.

Tulsi was yelling for the ball on the edge of the penalty area. TJ hit his cross hard and low, but it never reached Tulsi. Rafi was racing forward and the ball hit him on the knee. The deflection carried it past the stranded goalkeeper and into the net. 'What happened?' asked Rafi, as the crowd cheered.

'You scored,' said TJ.

'Did I? Rats! I didn't even see it.'

Seconds later the ref blew his whistle, and Parkview had won their first match of the tournament.

But they'd only won it by luck.

# CHAPTER 17

Parkview's second game was against Belford School. They won it easily, with TJ and Jay scoring a goal each. Jamie didn't have to make a single save. 'Does that mean we're through?' TJ asked when the match was over.

'I'm afraid not,' said Marshall. 'I've just been watching the other match in your group. Saint Joseph's beat Swinburne two nil. They're a good team.'

'And they beat Belford two nil as well,' Rob put in. 'So that means you have to beat them to get into the quarterfinals. A draw

isn't good enough because they have a
superior goal difference.'

# District Tournament
## Group table after 2 matches

|  | F | A | Points |
|---|---|---|---|
| St. Joseph's | 4 | 0 | 6 |
| Parkview | 3 | 0 | 6 |
| Swinburne | 0 | 3 | 0 |
| Belford | 0 | 4 | 0 |

## Results

| | | | |
|---|---|---|---|
| Swinburne | 0 | Parkview | 1 |
| Parkview | 2 | Belford | 0 |
| St. Joseph's | 2 | Swinburne | 0 |
| Belford | 0 | St. Joseph's | 2 |

'You're going to have to move the ball quicker,' Mr Wood told them. 'I know you've all been feeling nervous, but you've had two games to warm up now, so let's think about the things we've been practising. If you can see a first-time pass, then go for it. And, Jamie, try and catch them out when you have the ball. See if you can roll it out fast, before they're ready. OK, everyone, let's go.'

TJ could feel the urgency in the air. If they lost this game then they would be out of the tournament, and TJ still felt as if the tournament hadn't really started. He knew they'd all be disappointed if they didn't get at least to the quarterfinals.

Saint Joseph's kicked off and TJ knew at once that they were going to have to play far, far better than they had until now if they were going to beat them.

Their captain was a small midfielder called Mac, with hair that was even redder than Tommy's. He dribbled past Rafi and rode a tackle from Rodrigo, then played the ball out to the left wing, where the winger had a clear run down the touchline.

He crossed the ball and one of the Saint Joseph's strikers volleyed it fiercely at Jamie's goal. He dived to his right and the ball stuck to his hands as if he'd covered them with glue. He leaped to his feet and rolled the ball to Tommy, who flicked it instantly on to TJ. The Saint Joseph's players were racing back, but TJ hit a low first-time pass right across the field to Rafi. TJ felt a surge of energy running through him. This was real football.

Tulsi was standing in her usual position near the opposition penalty spot. She still didn't move as much as she should, TJ thought, but sometimes that didn't matter – like now. Because Rafi hit a pass into Tulsi's feet, and she did what she did best. She killed the ball with her right foot, shielding it from the defender who was breathing down her neck, then she pushed it a metre to the side, turned, and hit a low shot that sizzled past the goalkeeper.

She threw her arms in the air in her trademark celebration, standing still and grinning while the Parkview cheerleaders hurled a storm of blue-and-black pom-poms into the air.

'Hey!' yelled Rodrigo. 'Concentrate. We not won match. Only begin.'

'That's the most you've ever said,' TJ laughed, as they jogged back into their own half.

But Rodrigo's face was grim. He was their captain again for this match, and he had his job to do. 'They good team,' he said, clapping his hands. 'We work hard.'

Rodrigo was right. Saint Joseph's were a very good team. They seemed to be able to find each other with their passes without even looking. It was as if they could read each other's minds, and for long periods after they had taken the lead, Parkview didn't even touch the ball. It was Jamie who saved them. He worked as hard as anyone on the team, diving to the left and the right, throwing himself at the feet of attackers. St Joseph's won a whole string of corners, but every time Jamie leaped into the air and grabbed the ball above the heads of the attackers.

'I can't believe it's only half time,' TJ said at the interval. 'I feel as if I've run miles.'

'Well done, Jamie,' said Mr Wood, patting him on the back.

'Stunning!' said Marshall.

'They had eleven shots,' Rob said. 'All of them on target, and all of them saved.'

'Well, we're going to have to make some changes for the second half,' Mr Wood told them. 'TJ and Tommy, I'm taking you off.' He held up a hand to stop their protests.

'You've both done a lot of running, and remember, if we're going to win this tournament we'll have to play three more matches after this one. Besides, we can always bring you back on if we need to. Tulsi, you stay upfield. If they manage to clear the ball to you, your job is to hold it up until the midfield can join you. Understood?'

'It's a risky strategy,' Rob said to TJ, as the teams took the field again. 'We're going to defend most of the time, and Jamie's sure to let one in eventually.'

'We were defending most of the time in the first half,' Tommy pointed out. 'It'll be easier with more defenders.'

TJ said nothing. He was fed up that Mr Wood had taken him off. He was sure he could have scored another goal and made the game safe. And now he could only watch, as Saint Joseph's continued to press forward and pepper Jamie's goal with shots.

The end of the match drew near. Parkview only had to hold out for a few seconds more. Mr Wood and Marshall were both looking at their watches. Some of the Parkview supporters were covering their eyes and screaming every time another shot came in. Rodrigo managed to tackle the red-haired Mac, but instantly another Saint Joseph's player was on to him. He could only pass sideways to Leila, and the only thing she could do was play the ball back to Jamie.

'Don't pick it up!' yelled Rob. 'It's a back pass,' he said, turning to TJ. 'He has to kick it.'

'Oh, no,' groaned TJ, as Jamie took two

steps forward. 'This might go anywhere.' He sighed with relief as the clearance flew over the heads of all the attackers. On the halfway line Tulsi was waiting, marked by the defender who hadn't left her side for the whole game. He had made one mistake to let her score, and now he made another. He should have stepped forward and headed the ball away, but instead he decided to let it bounce. He stepped back, getting ready to clear it, and Tulsi saw her chance. As the ball hit the ground she controlled it with one touch and then flicked it between the legs of the stranded defender. A perfect nutmeg!

While the defender was still wondering what had happened, she sprinted forward and buried the ball in the net. Parkview were through to the quarterfinals.

# CHAPTER 18

Parkview won their quarterfinal 4 – 0, with two goals apiece for Tulsi and TJ. It was a very one-sided game and Jamie didn't have to make a single save. 'It's weird,' he said after the game. 'If we play against a really good team then I have loads to do, but if we play brilliantly then it's boring. I mean, it's just like watching from the touchline.'

'No, it's not,' said Rob. 'You can't just watch. You have to be ready all the time in case there's an attack.'

Jamie shook his head. 'You saw that game,' he said. 'They hardly even got in our half.'

'Would you like to know who you're play-ing in the semifinal?' Mr Wood said, smiling. 'It's Hillside. They've won all their matches so far, just like you.'

The Parkview players looked at each other. 'They've got this new player,' Tulsi said. 'He's Chinese. He's called Deng.'

'And he's completely brilliant,' said Jamie. 'We played them in the park and they beat us twenty-three two.'

'You know what?' Marshall said. 'It's about time you guys started believing in yourselves. As far as I can see, you already beat the best team in the tournament – Saint Joseph's. You put them out! And you did that without even playing that well. You've got a great team and you've got a great coach. And great supporters too,' he added, with a glance at the far touchline, where the cheerleaders were having a wonderful time. 'Go out there and really

show them what you can do. Just look.
I reckon your whole school is here!'

TJ looked. What Marshall said was true.
During the morning the crowd had been
swelling. Whole families were there, with
lots of little kids running around playing
football. And all the teachers were there too,
even Mrs Logan, the deputy head. And Mr
Coggins, of course. Mr Burrows was walking
towards them now, with a tall grey-haired
man who looked somehow familiar.
Mr Burrows looked unusually cheerful. 'You
remember Mr Turvey?' he said, and TJ found
it hard to recognize the inspector without his
grey suit on.

'I wanted to see what was so special
about this football team that seems to
have turned your whole school around,'
Mr Turvey said with a smile. 'Good luck in
your semifinal, everyone!'

The referee was waiting. 'OK,' said

Mr Wood. 'Jamie in goal, Leila and Tommy at the back, then Rodrigo and Rafi, and TJ and Tulsi up front. You know what to do.'

# Parkview Team Sheet

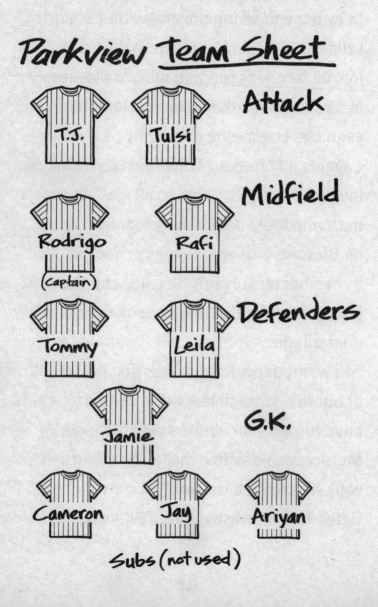

**Attack**
T.J.
Tulsi

**Midfield**
Rodrigo
(captain)
Rafi

**Defenders**
Tommy
Leila

**G.K.**
Jamie

Cameron
Jay
Ariyan

Subs (not used)

TJ looked at Deng, as they took up their positions. He was still grinning, as if someone had just told him a very funny joke. 'Why are you all looking so worried?' said Leila.

'You haven't seen him play,' Rafi told her.

'But we've got Jamie in goal now,' Leila said. 'He won't let them score.'

Jamie blushed, and the Parkview players laughed. Suddenly TJ felt a million times better. 'We can win this,' he called. 'Come on, Parkview!'

The Parkview supporters took up the chant. 'PARKVIEW!' they yelled, as the dinner ladies and the cooks went into a complicated routine. 'COME ON, PARKVIEW!'

Krissy Barton kicked off, and the barrel-shaped Kelvin played the ball out to Slim, the Hillside captain, who was playing on the wing. He pushed the ball back towards Deng. The pass was hit well enough, but Rafi was on fire. He darted in and stole the ball before Deng could reach it, and passed to Leila, who moved it on to TJ.

Instantly Deng moved over to try and cut off his run, and TJ knew that this was like a duel between the two of them. If he could beat Deng, if he could put doubt and fear into Deng's heart, then it would change the game completely. So he ran at Deng, with the ball at his feet, and Deng backed off, watching the ball closely. TJ feinted to go inside Deng, and at the last moment played the ball outside him with his left foot. Deng saw what was happening and his right foot flashed out, but the ball had already gone.

TJ felt a spike of pain as Deng's boot clipped his ankle, but he didn't go down. He knew that this was a big chance. He jumped over Deng's outstretched leg and struggled for a moment to keep his balance. The ball was running towards the touchline, and with a desperate stretch, TJ managed to keep it in play.

Now he was free. Deng was on the ground and would never catch him. As he raced for the dead-ball line, he looked across and saw Tulsi taking up her usual position near the penalty spot. Two of the Hillside players had gone with her, leaving plenty of space for Rafi to burst forward, completely unmarked.

TJ hit a perfectly weighted pass. Somehow he knew exactly how hard to strike the ball so that it would arrive at the perfect moment for Rafi to make the shot. And it did. Rafi hit a scorching drive that TJ was pretty sure even Jamie wouldn't have stopped.

'I meant that one!' Rafi said, as he exchanged high-fives with TJ and the Parkview fans began singing again. 'Great pass, TJ. Amazing run too. That showed them!'

For the rest of the first half, the game was evenly balanced. Jamie had to make two saves from Kelvin's shots, and once Tulsi managed a long-range effort, but every spectator was riveted by the battle between TJ and Deng. When Deng had seen TJ's cross converted by Rafi, he'd climbed to his feet with the grin still on his face, and begun to shadow TJ everywhere he went. Every time TJ received the ball, Deng was there. If TJ tried to beat him, Deng's boot snaked out and won the ball. If TJ made a run, Deng tracked him all the way. 'I don't know what to do,' TJ said at half time. 'He never gives me a second.'

'Just keep at it,' Mr Wood told him. 'This is when fitness is going to start to make a real difference. Hillside have had some hard games. Deng's going to tire. You can make it worse for him by keeping up those runs when you don't have the ball. You're fast, TJ, and you've been training hard. Now make it count.'

TJ did as Mr Wood had suggested. He made runs right back inside his own half, calling for the ball from the defenders and playing it back to them, then turning and making new runs down the wing. Every time, Deng came with him. TJ thought his lungs were going to burst, as he saw Krissy inter-cept a pass and hit a shot at Jamie. TJ raced back, forcing his legs to keep moving, and now, at last, he realized that he'd left Deng gasping behind him. 'Here, Jamie!' he called. 'Give it to me.'

Jamie rolled the ball to his feet and TJ took it forward a few metres, and space suddenly opened up ahead of him. Deng had turned and was following doggedly, but TJ was certain now that Deng couldn't keep up with him. As he ran forward, Tulsi was heading towards the edge of the penalty area, while Rafi was moving quickly through the centre circle. Two of the Hillside players had followed Rafi. There was nothing between TJ and the Hillside goal. He felt as if he was flying, as if he could run for ever.

As the goalkeeper came out, TJ slid the ball underneath him and he knew – he just knew – that they were going to win the match. Parkview were going through to the final!

# CHAPTER 19

'That was fabulous, TJ,' Marshall said after the game. 'Just a terrific performance. And a great game to watch.' Marshall had been out on the pitch and shaken hands with every one of the Hillside players, so now everyone knew that Marshall was here. He'd even taken off his hoodie, and TJ knew that people were watching them. 'The whole team did great,' continued Marshall. 'But it was you running Deng into the ground that made the difference.'

TJ smiled with satisfaction. Deng had shaken his hand after the game. 'You were just too good,' he'd said. 'I don't know how you kept going like that. I'm shattered.'

'You remember Phil, don't you, TJ?' Marshall asked him. 'He's from Wanderers. He showed you around when you visited.'

TJ could see now why he hadn't recognized Phil before. His puffa jacket and hat made him look fat, and a lot older than he was, and now TJ realized that Phil was the man who'd been at the Wasps match. The one everyone had said was a scout.

'I come to all these tournaments,' Phil said. 'And a lot of Sunday League games. We're always on the lookout for talent. That lad, Deng, for instance,' he said, with a twinkle in his eye. 'I've been watching him for a while. Good luck in the final. You're going to have your work cut out.'

'What did he mean?' asked TJ, as Phil walked away.

'Didn't you know?' said TJ's dad. 'You're

playing Meadow Green. They won their semi-final five nil. They're playing out of their skins!'

'Get some rest, everyone,' said Mr Wood. 'The final is at two o'clock, so you've got time to have something to eat and drink too. Not too much, mind. Remember what happened to the Wasps. They won't be making that mistake again.'

'Here, TJ,' said his mum. 'I've got you a wrap with chicken and salad. And some juice. You must be starving after all that running.'

TJ realized that it was true. He finished the wrap quickly. 'I could eat that all over again,' he said.

'Well, don't,' said his brother Joey. 'But maybe you should go and check up on Jamie.'

A short distance away Jamie was laughing and joking with his family. And eating. TJ's heart sank. If Jamie ate too much it would be a disaster. 'What are you doing?' TJ said to him. 'Didn't you hear what Mr Wood said?'

Jamie was lifting a large piece of pork pie to his mouth. 'Now then, TJ,' said Jamie's mum. 'You let him be. One piece of pie's not going to do any harm.'

'And the rest,' said TJ, looking at the tell-tale crumbs on Jamie's plate.

Jamie put the pie down. 'It's all right for you,' he said. 'You've got a scout from Wanderers watching you. I'm just a goalie. And I'm famished.'

'He's not watching me—' began TJ. Then he stopped, remembering the look that had passed between Marshall and Phil.

'Of course he is,' Jamie said. 'Everybody knows. But anyway, I don't have to run like you do, and I've been starving myself for weeks.'

'Please, Jamie. You want to win the final, don't you?'

Jamie looked at TJ, then he looked at the pie. Finally he handed the plate to little Max.

'Here,' he said. 'You share this with Cody. Me and TJ are going to get some practice.'

As TJ hit shots at Jamie, they could see the crowd gathering around the pitch where the final was going to be played. Meadow Green had almost as many supporters as Parkview.

'We wouldn't be in the final if it wasn't for you,' TJ said to Jamie. 'All those saves you made.'

'I'm sort of getting used to it,' Jamie replied, as he caught one of TJ's fierce drives easily and bowled it back to him. 'I mean, in a way the goalie is the ultimate defender, isn't he?'

TJ laughed. 'Just make sure you keep your eye on the ball when you're kicking it out,' he said.

'I've been practising,' Jamie told him confidently. 'I won't make a mistake.'

TJ looked at him. That was Jamie, he thought. He was someone you could rely on – as long as food wasn't involved. And actually Jamie had probably had a harder job than any of them to get fit. But he'd done it.

'Come on,' said Jamie. 'It's time.'

Rodrigo ran to the centre of the pitch and shook hands with Leroy. Leroy won the toss.

'Good luck, everyone,' said the ref. 'Let's have a great game for all these spectators.'

There was rope running along the touchline to keep the spectators back, but behind the rope people were crowded three or four deep. Both sets of supporters were shouting at the tops of their voices.

Suddenly TJ was desperate for the match to begin. He didn't feel nervous any more. He felt full of energy, and he wanted to run.

Then the whistle blew and the final of the District Tournament was under way.

Meadow Green attacked hard. Several times they pressed forward and hit shots that fizzed just wide or over the bar. But Parkview gave as good as they got. Tulsi had a long-range shot saved, and once TJ was nearly through on goal when the black-haired defender made an incredible tackle.

Then Leroy punched the ball out to little Martin on the left wing, and Martin took on Rodrigo before hitting a clever pass into the path of Meadow Green's blond-haired striker. He took the ball on his right foot and smashed his way past Tommy before un-leashing a thunderous shot. Jamie dived to his right and just managed to push the ball onto the post. It rebounded from the post, hit Jamie and rolled towards the line. There were gasps from the crowd as he hurled himself backwards and grabbed the ball at the last possible moment.

Jamie stood up, grinning, and rolled the

ball to Tommy. Now it was Parkview's turn to attack as Tommy moved forward and played a precise pass down the line for TJ to chase.

It was just what TJ had been waiting for. It was a race between him and the defender, and he never doubted that he would win. He felt as if he could outrun anyone, and the pass was brilliant. He didn't even have to break his stride as he picked up the ball, swerved inside the last defender and curled the ball around the goalkeeper, just inside the post.

# TJ first goal in the final

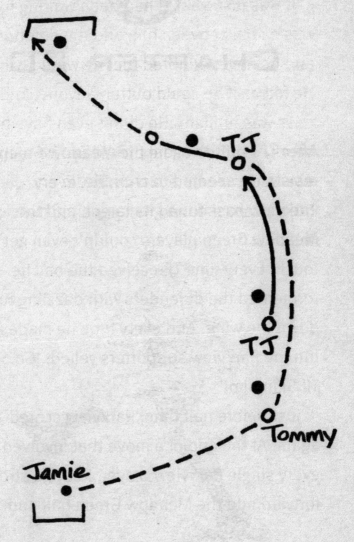

# CHAPTER 20

After TJ's brilliant goal the Meadow Green resistance seemed to crumble. Every Parkview pass found its target, and the Meadow Green players couldn't even get a touch. Every time TJ received the ball he tormented the defenders with dazzling runs down the wing. And every time he made a run the Parkview supporters yelled, 'Go on, TJ! Skin him!'

Just before half time, Parkview scored again. At the end of a move that involved every single Parkview player, Rodrigo strode forward into the Meadow Green half and launched a powerful shot from nearly thirty metres out. The ball was still rising when it hit the back of the net. All the Parkview players ran to Rodrigo, and their supporters began to chant, 'WE'RE GONNA WIN THE CUP! WE'RE GONNA WIN THE CUP!'

Even Jamie ran out from his goal to clap Rodrigo on the back. Rodrigo jumped up and down with excitement and punched the air, and TJ could hear Rodrigo's dad yelling, 'Gol! Gol! Gol! Goooooooooooooal!!!'

We're going to win, TJ thought, as Meadow Green kicked off. We'll be District Champions. He was already dreaming of lifting the trophy into the air. He looked across and saw Tulsi waving to her gran, who was dancing around on the touchline.

Rodrigo was still beaming and laughing with Tommy. Then TJ heard Jamie screaming, 'Look out, you idiots! They've kicked off!'

It was as if someone had thrown a bucket

of cold water at him. The Meadow Green players were streaming forward, but the Parkview team had woken up far too late.

The blond-haired striker was through, and Jamie was desperately trying to spread himself, but it was no good, because Leroy was running free. The striker slid the ball to him and he slotted it home. 2–1!

The Meadow Green fans erupted, but on the Parkview side there was an eerie silence, before Janice and the dinner ladies slowly started chanting again, and gradually the whole crowd began to join in. In the middle of all the noise, Meadow Green attacked again and again, forcing Jamie to make two more saves before the whistle blew for half time.

'You made a stupid mistake,' said Mr Wood. 'You all switched off. But even Premier League teams do it. Even Wanderers, right, Marshall?'

'It's true,' said Marshall. 'You've done great, but you thought you'd won it already, right?'

They all nodded despondently. 'Well, you have to put it behind you,' Marshall continued. 'You were outplaying them before they scored, and you can outplay them again. You're still one goal ahead. But remember – you haven't won the game until the ref blows the final whistle!'

When they ran back onto the pitch TJ could see the determination on everyone's faces. He heard Marshall's voice yelling, 'Come on, Parkview! You can do it!'

It was a very close match now. The play swung from one end to the other. Both goal-keepers made great saves and both teams put together sparkling moves that ended in narrow misses. The crowd gasped and roared and groaned. It was a wonderful game to watch.

Time was ticking away, as Tulsi played the ball out to Rafi, who had run wide. Rafi laid the ball back to Rodrigo. The blond-haired striker tried to tackle Rodrigo, who side-stepped and cleared the ball towards Tulsi.

Just at that moment she saw the ref look at his watch. She took her eye off the ball and she controlled it badly. Leroy pounced, looked up, and saw the blond-haired striker racing forward. He hit a high, curling pass over the striker's shoulder, but Tommy was alert to the danger.

As the striker took the ball into the penalty area, Tommy was matching him stride for stride. He timed his challenge perfectly, and hooked the ball to safety. Both Tommy and the striker tumbled to the ground in a heap.

TJ breathed a sigh of relief.

Then he heard the gasps from the

Parkview fans. The linesman was waving his flag in the air. The ref ran over to him, listened for a moment, then turned and pointed to the penalty spot.

# CHAPTER 21

TJ felt himself trembling. It seemed so unfair. He could hear mutterings of discontent from the Parkview supporters, but then Janice began to shout. 'JAMIE! JAMIE!'

'Go for it, Jamie, you can do it,' yelled Leila and the other subs.

Tommy tried to get to his feet, but as he put his weight on his leg it seemed to collapse underneath him. Mr Wood raced onto the pitch and Rob followed him carrying Mr Wood's bag. All the Parkview players gathered in the penalty area. 'Sorry, everyone,' said Tulsi, as they waited.

'I should have been ready.'

'None of us were ready,' TJ said. 'And now this. It was never a penalty.'

'It doesn't matter,' Rob said. 'You can save it, Jamie. Leroy takes their penalties. He's taken three today already, and each one was the same. Low to the left. That's your right,' he added, to Jamie, just to be sure. 'I asked one of the Meadow Green parents and she said he always does the same.'

'Hold on,' said Jamie. 'How many of them did he score?'

'I was hoping you wouldn't ask me that,' Rob replied.

'He scored all of them, didn't he?' said Jamie, shaking his head.

'But you weren't the goalie,' said Rob. 'Just go for it. Low to your right.'

Mr Wood helped Tommy off the pitch and Leila ran on to take his place. 'Tough luck,

Tommy,' she said, as she ran past him. 'That was a great tackle.'

Leroy placed the ball on the spot, then stood up and looked Jamie in the eye. Jamie stared back at him, and spread his arms wide, bouncing on the balls of his feet. TJ remembered suddenly how unfit Jamie had been a few short weeks ago. Back then Jamie could never have saved a penalty, but now he looked like a big cat, ready to pounce.

The crowd fell silent as the referee's whistle blew. Leroy's run-up seemed to happen in slow motion. As he struck the ball, Jamie was already diving to his right. The ball flew hard and low. It was going in, right inside the post, but then, at the last possible moment, Jamie was there, stretching full-length like an Olympic diver to grab the ball with both hands. He bounced to his feet and ran to the edge of the area, waving the Parkview players forward, as he rolled the ball into Leila's path. She slid a pass to Rafi. TJ was running to the left, away from the goal, taking a defender with him. Then he turned suddenly, calling to Rafi, running back towards the centre just the way they'd practised at the Wanderers training ground.

Rafi understood at once and played the ball in to TJ's feet. He passed it first time to Tulsi and followed his pass, as Tulsi laid the ball back to him.

It was perfect! TJ's shot hit the back of the net before the keeper could move.

TJ pulled his shirt over his face and ran round in circles until Rafi caught up with him and lifted him off the ground. And in the middle of the Parkview celebrations the referee blew his whistle a second time. The match was over, and now Parkview School really were the District Champions.

On the touchline, Mr Burrows and Mr Coggins had borrowed pom-poms from the dinner ladies and were waving them madly.

The Meadow Green players fell to their knees, but they cheered up a little when Marshall came onto the pitch and talked to them and shook their hands. 'You're dead lucky having Marshall Jones helping you,' Leroy said when TJ shook hands with him. 'Maybe I could come to your school.'

'Yeah, but you might not get in the team,' laughed TJ. Then he saw the look on Leroy's face. 'I'm kidding,' he said. 'Of course you would. You were brilliant today.'

The Meadow Green striker came over to Tommy. 'Are you OK?' he asked. 'It was a great tackle. That linesman needs glasses.'

'Right,' said Rodrigo. 'Ref needs a glass!'

'He's from Portugal,' said Tulsi.

Tommy grinned. 'It didn't matter in the end,' he said. 'Thanks to Jamie.'

Jamie was completely surrounded by excited Parkview supporters who were all moving towards the table where the trophies and medals were arranged. 'It was a magnificent final,' said a white-haired man who was in charge. 'Two evenly matched teams, and a fair result in the end. We have a very special guest today, so I'm going to ask Marshall Jones to present the medals. First of all, the runners-up. Meadow Green School.'

There was a huge cheer from the crowd and loud applause for every Meadow Green player. Then it was Parkview's turn. One at a time they went forward to receive their medals, and there was an especially big cheer for Jamie. Marshall handed the trophy to Rodrigo and he lifted it high in the air to the biggest cheer of all.

TJ could see his family, and Jamie's and Tulsi's. There was Rob and his dad, and all the teachers and dinner ladies and cooks. It was everything he'd ever dreamed of. Even Danny was there, TJ realized with surprise, catching sight of his pale face through a gap in the crowd.

When the presentations were over, the Parkview team and their supporters gathered together under the trees.

'Phil would like a word with you, TJ,' said Mr Wood with a smile. 'And you too, Jamie. And your mums and dads.'

'Well done today, lads,' Phil said. 'How would you feel about coming along to our Player Development Centre on Wednesday nights? I've had my eye on you, TJ. But Jamie, you were a big surprise. I think you could be a great goalkeeper one day. What do you think? Will you come?'

TJ couldn't speak. 'Of course he will,'

said his mum.

Jamie just looked stunned. 'But . . . but . . .
I'm not really a goalkeeper,' he stammered.
'I mean, do you really mean it? Me?'

'Trust me, Jamie,' said Phil. 'It's my job
to watch out for talent, and you have it,
believe me.'

'Well, thanks,' Jamie said. He scratched
his head and his face broke into the biggest
smile TJ had ever seen. 'I'd rather be a great
goalkeeper than a dodgy defender any day.
When do we start?'

Suddenly everyone was talking at once.
TJ and Jamie just stared at each other and
smiled stupidly. It was great to be picked
out by Phil, thought TJ, but it was just
fantastic that his friend had been chosen
too.

'Now wait a minute,' said Mrs Hubbard,
the school cook, pushing her way through
the crowd with an enormous box in her

arms. 'I had a feeling that young Jamie was going to save the day, and I knew we'd win. So I made a little something to celebrate.'

She put the box down on the grass and lifted out a gigantic cake in the shape of a football. She cut a huge slice. 'Here you are, Jamie love,' she said. 'You must be starving after all that diving around. Tuck in! You deserve it.'

At the back of the crowd someone started chanting, 'JAMIE! JAMIE!'

Everyone laughed and began to join in. 'Go on, Jamie,' said TJ. 'You can do it!'

Jamie lifted the cake to his lips. It was oozing with sticky icing and jam and cream. He took a giant mouthful, closed his eyes and smiled.

'Mmmmmm!' he said. 'I'll go in goal for ever if I can have cake like that after every match.'

# Final Table

|              | F | A | Points |
|--------------|---|---|--------|
| Parkview     | 5 | 0 | 9      |
| St. Joseph's | 4 | 2 | 6      |
| Swinburne    | 2 | 3 | 3      |
| Belford      | 0 | 6 | 0      |

## Results

| Parkview  | 2 | St. Joseph's | 0 |
|-----------|---|--------------|---|
| Swinburne | 2 | Belford      | 0 |

# THEO WALCOTT

**THEO WALCOTT** was born on 16th March 1989 and grew up near Newbury. After joining the youth scheme at Southampton, he became the Saints' youngest ever player, before joining Arsenal in January 2006.

Following Theo's surprise selection in Sven-Göran Eriksson's World Cup squad, Theo set another record in making his England debut at the age of just 17 years and 75 days, and was named the BBC's Young Sports Personality of the Year in 2006.

Theo is now a star player for both Arsenal and England and in September 2008 became the youngest player to score a hat-trick for England.

**Don't miss any of the action
with TJ and his team-mates!**

## T.J. AND THE HAT-TRICK

### BY THEO WALCOTT

TJ couldn't believe he'd never played
football before. It was such a great game!
But with nowhere to play and no one to
coach them, TJ and his new friends at
Parkview are worried that they'll never get
a proper team together. The head teacher
even threatens to ban football.

TJ and his football-mad friends know they
can't let that happen. Then Mr Wood arrives
and things really start to look up . . .

978 0 552 56245 4

Coming soon . . .

# T.J. AND THE CUP RUN

## BY THEO WALCOTT

TJ and his friends get a terrible shock
when their old teacher, Mr Potter, returns
from illness to take over from Mr Wood as
PE teacher at Parkview School. Worse still,
they are about to play in the semifinal of
the Cup, and Mr Potter's really bad tactics
nearly lose them the match.

With everything they've trained for
hanging in the balance, can TJ and his
friends turn things around and win?

978 0 552 56247 8

**Coming soon . . .**

# T.J. AND THE
# WINNING GOAL

## BY THEO WALCOTT

The Parkview team are off to compete in the
Regional Championship tournament, but their
striker is in trouble. The team is improving
all the time, but Tulsi, once the star, is getting
left behind. When she's dropped from both the
school team and her Sunday League team, she
even talks about giving up football.

Can TJ and the team help Tulsi change her
ways and win her place back in the team?

978 0 552 56248 5